James Pattinson is a full-time author who, despite having travelled throughout the world, still lives in the remote village where he grew up. He has written magazine articles, short stories and radio features as well as numerous novels.

BULLION

Alan Caley was far from delighted to receive a phone call from his old school pal Chuck Brogan, suggesting that the two of them should get together for lunch. It was quite some time since he had last seen Brogan — the man had been sent to prison for a number of years for taking part in a bullion robbery. Caley felt inclined to refuse the invitation, but Brogan hinted that the meeting might be to Caley's advantage — financially. And Caley could surely use some help in that respect. So he agreed to have lunch with Brogan, little suspecting what dire consequences were to stem from that free meal.

JAMES PATTINSON

BULLION

Complete and Unabridged

ULVERSCROFT
Leicester

Published in Great Britain in 2004 by
Robert Hale Limited
London

First Large Print Edition
published 2005
by arrangement with
Robert Hale Limited
London

British Library CIP Data

Pattinson, James, *1915* –
    Bullion.—Large print ed.—
    Ulverscroft large print series: adventure & suspense
    1. Suspense fiction
    2. Large type books
    I. Title
    823.9'14 [F]

    ISBN 1–84395–624–1

Published by
F. A. Thorpe (Publishing)
Anstey, Leicestershire

Set by Words & Graphics Ltd.
Anstey, Leicestershire
Printed and bound in Great Britain by
T. J. International Ltd., Padstow, Cornwall

This book is printed on acid-free paper

Contents

1

Old Acquaintance

The voice on the telephone sounded vaguely familiar to Caley, yet he could not quite place it. It was like an echo from the past; maybe a past he had no wish to be reminded of.

'Long time no see, Alan old boy,' the voice said. 'Too long. Now why don't you and me get together sometime? Soon. Must have a lot to talk about.'

'Is that so?' Caley said.

And still he had not placed the voice. Who the devil was it calling him?

There were some people like this one, who never bothered to introduce themselves; expected you to know straightaway who was talking, even though maybe you had met them only a couple of times. It annoyed Caley. He felt like telling the man to say who he was or ring off, because he was no good at guessing games.

It was certainly a man. Unless it was a woman with a remarkably gruff voice. And this seemed unlikely.

But then the caller gave a laugh and said:

'You don't know who I am, do you?'

'No, I don't,' Caley said.

'Well, I suppose it's not surprising. It's been a while. Yes, quite a while. Unfortunately.'

Caley failed to see why it should have been unfortunate. But he said nothing; just waited for the other man to go on. Which, after a brief pause, he did.

'Give you a clue. Chuck.'

Caley got it then. 'Chuck Brogan!'

The man gave another laugh. 'As ever was.'

Caley began remembering things then. Some of them he would have preferred to leave forgotten. He had been at school with Brogan; and that must have been all of twenty years ago. They had been pals of a sort, off and on, but had lost touch long since, with no regrets on Caley's part. Because Brogan had been a bad hat, no doubt about it; the kind of man it was wise not to become too closely involved with.

He remembered more; things that had happened long after he had lost touch with Brogan and been only too thankful that he had. Brogan had got himself into the news, front page stuff; and for all the wrong reasons.

There had been this big bullion robbery, amounting to millions, and Brogan's picture had been published all over the place; because he had been one of the gang; the only one in fact that had ever been nailed.

The gold had never been recovered. It was believed that Brogan could have told where it was if he had wished. He had been picked up driving a white Ford van, and close examination of this vehicle revealed irrefutable evidence that it had recently carried gold. There were traces of the precious metal remaining in it, though none of the ingots were there. There was also a balaclava helmet which he had been foolish enough not to throw away. It was known that the robbers had been wearing balaclavas because two of them had been left at the scene of the crime.

All through his trial Brogan had staunchly denied having taken any part in the bullion heist, during which a night-watchman had been seriously injured; but he had been unable to provide an alibi and there had been enough circumstantial evidence to convict him. As a result he had gone out of circulation for a number of years, and if Caley had wished to have a meeting with him he would have had to pay a visit to one of Her Majesty's prisons. Not that he had felt any such desire; far from it. The less he saw of Brogan the better, from his point of view. Old school pal or not, the man was poison.

Yet here he was at this very moment on the telephone proposing a meeting and saying they had a lot to talk about. Well, that last part of it might be true. There was the bullion robbery for one thing. Indeed, the main thing, and possibly the only thing of any importance. But could that really be a subject Brogan would want to talk about, since he had always denied having anything to do with it? Unfortunately for him, apart from the fact that he could produce no credible alibi, he had been unable to give a good explanation as to why he had been driving around the countryside in a white van in the small hours of the morning. All very suspicious, especially when allied to those slight traces of gold discovered in the vehicle. Not to mention the balaclava.

'So how about it?' Brogan said.

Caley evinced no enthusiasm for the idea. 'Oh, I really don't know — '

'Sure you do. What you got against it?'

'Well — '

'Ah, I see how it is. You reckon I'm a bad character you'd rather not be seen hobnobbing with. Is that it?'

'No,' Caley said. But it was. Brogan had hit the nail on the head and they both knew it.

'Tell you something,' Brogan said. 'It could be to your advantage.'

Caley failed to see how that might be. Though he could not deny to himself that something to his advantage, especially if it involved an injection of hard cash, might be more than acceptable, seeing the way his financial affairs stood at the present time. The possibility that Brogan might be in a position to give him any assistance in that respect seemed, however, to be remote indeed.

'Look,' Brogan said. 'What have you got to lose? It'll be my treat.'

Caley thought about it. So what did he have to lose? His reputation if he was seen hanging around with a character like Chuck Brogan? What reputation for Pete's sake? And if Brogan was paying it would be a free meal; which as matters stood with him at the present time was not to be sniffed at.

So he said: 'Well, maybe we could think of something to talk about if we put our minds to it.'

'Sure we could. Plenty. So it's on, is it?'

'I suppose so. When and where?'

Brogan had evidently got it all planned out already. 'Tomorrow. Make it twelve-thirty, if that's all right with you. There's a half-decent place called the Top Notch, so I've heard. You know it?'

'No. Where is it?'

'It's out your way. Well, sort of. Not West

5

End. You'll find it easy. Look it up in the Yellow Pages. I'll book a table.'

Caley doubted whether a restaurant chosen by Chuck Brogan would be anywhere near the top flight, but he let it pass. He felt he was being dragged into something he might live to regret, and he had an impulse to change his mind, call the whole thing off before it was too late. But that would have seemed stupid. And in spite of his misgivings he could not help feeling somewhat intrigued. Brogan had hinted at rather more than a mere exchange of reminiscences, and he wanted to know what it was. Especially if it really should turn out to be to his advantage.

'So that's settled,' Brogan said. 'Half-past twelve tomorrow at the Top Notch. Right?'

'I suppose so.'

'Right then,' Brogan said. 'Be seeing you.'

And he rang off.

2

No Patter of Tiny Feet

Caley put the telephone down and lit a cigarette. He had only recently started smoking again after having kicked the habit for a couple of years. And this was really a stupid thing to do, because when matters were going badly and you were having difficulty in seeing where the next pound was coming from the expense of smoking with cigarettes at the price they were today was hardly calculated to help the situation. But to hell with it! At least he had not gone on the bottle. That really would have been crazy.

He felt depressed; and what with one thing and another he had reason to be. It was growing dark, but there was enough light remaining to see from the window of the room which he called his office the yard and the somewhat dilapidated outhouses. The Ford pick-up truck was standing there; the only means of transport he had now that the Volvo and the two remaining lorries had been sold. In one corner was a heap of sand, and there were a few piles of bricks, tiles, drainpipes and other odds and ends of building material, all looking rather abandoned and forlorn.

For until quite recently this had been the site of a builders' merchant, and that merchant had been Alan Caley. There had been a time in the early days when it had been a reasonably thriving business which he had taken over from his father, and he had had great hopes for its future. But somehow, and he still did not understand quite why, trade had fallen away and the time had come when he could no longer conceal from himself the dismal fact that he was heading for the rocks.

He had avoided bankruptcy only because he had seen in time the way the wind was blowing. It had been a hard decision to make, but he had made it. He had stopped trading, had collected as much as he could of the money that was owed him by various jobbing builders, some of whom were in a similar situation to his but were hanging on by their fingernails, and shut up shop.

The result of these concluding financial transactions was that he was left still in possession of his property, such as it was, and enough cash in the bank to keep him going for the present. Meanwhile he would have to look around for some alternative means of scratching a living.

This, of course, had not been good enough for his wife, and he had never imagined it would be.

'What,' she demanded, 'am I expected to do? Live on a measly pittance?'

Caley had no satisfactory answer to that. Martine, thirty-five, blonde and still attractive even if not quite the beauty she had once been, was fond of the good things in life: expensive clothes, jewellery, parties, that kind of thing. He had never said as much to her, but the fact could not be denied that her expensive lifestyle had, at least in part, contributed to the failure of the business. She had been a constant drain on the cash supply, and any suggestion on his part that she might put some curb on her extravagance had been met with withering scorn.

'So I'm to penny-pinch just because you're too bloody incompetent to run a successful business. Is that it?'

Caley could only shrug. Sometimes he wondered why she had married him. It could hardly have been described as a match made in heaven. He was five years older than her and with no pretensions to the kind of looks that might have made him a star on the silver screen, even if he could have managed the acting. The best that could have been said of

9

him was that there was nothing truly repulsive about him. He was just ordinary; one of the great majority: five feet eight in height, probably somewhat overweight, with thinning mousey hair and rather plump features. Recently he had grown a beard, but it was not a great success and he was thinking of shaving it off.

Martine had been scathing. 'Makes you look like an old billy-goat.'

Which hurt him more than he would have cared to admit.

Well, there would be no more insults from her now, because she had walked out on him; just packed her things and gone. He guessed she was living with her parents, but he did not bother to enquire. In a way it was a relief to be shot of her. At least he would no longer have her as a drain on his dwindling resources. Unless of course she came round with the begging-bowl.

★   ★   ★

Caley had taken over the business of builders' merchant from his father. The old man had been a shrewd operator and had made a success of it. Caley himself had worked in the office after leaving school and knew the way things were run. He was an only child and it

10

was more or less accepted that when his father eventually gave up he would take over the firm as a going concern. And that was the way it would probably have been if old Joe and his wife had not had this sudden hankering for a place in the sun where they could spend their declining years.

And where must they go to find the sun? Where but to Spain!

'We've earned it,' Joe said. 'Haven't we, Mother?'

'We certainly have,' Mother agreed.

And so it was settled. The son had no say in the matter. He had to take it or leave it. So he took it.

'You'll be all right, son,' his father assured him. 'There'll be enough working capital left for you to carry on the business and make a decent living. And you know it all. You can't lose.'

He had been wrong on that point of course.

★　★　★

Caley was already married to Martine. They had met at a dance-hall. He was not much of a dancer, but he had been persuaded to go by a young fellow named Wilf, one of his very few friends.

11

'You'll enjoy it,' Wilf said. 'There'll be lots of girls. You can take your pick.'

And of course there were lots of girls. And one of them was a certain Martine Jones.

'Well, there's a thing,' Wilf said. 'I know that girl. The one in the corner with the long blonde hair and the flashy earrings. What you think of her?'

'I think she's gorgeous,' Caley said. And he meant it.

'Want me to introduce you?'

'Oh, I don't know — '

'Sure you do,' Wilf said. 'Come on.'

★　★　★

That was how it had started. Caley had fallen in love with her from the moment he saw her. For her part she appeared to tolerate his attentions without any great show of passion. Much later, when they had been married for a year or two, he had long come to the conclusion that she had simply been on the lookout for a husband and he had come along at the right moment. Maybe she had wanted to get away from her family and be independent. Maybe too she had taken a look at Joe Caley's business and thought it looked prosperous; which of course it was at that time. She could have figured out that it would all come to Alan in the course of time and that she would be on easy street.

So much for human expectations!

★ ★ ★

After the marriage they had lived comfortably enough. Joe had had the first floor of the old rambling house converted into a self-contained flat with every modern convenience. Caley thought they could hardly have asked for more comfortable quarters, but Martine was always grumbling about one thing or another. She complained that it was poky — that was her word for it. But she complained about so many things. She seemed to be a complainer by nature.

Her chief complaint concerned the situation. Canning Town, she maintained, was really out in the sticks.

'There's no class about it, now is there?'

Caley wondered why she should have been so bothered about class, seeing that her father was the landlord of a public house in East Ham. But perhaps that was the kind of thing she had married in order to get away from.

'Well,' he said, 'it's within easy reach of the West End, so what more do you want?'

Quite a lot more, as it turned out: designer branded clothes, jewellery that was the genuine article and not the tawdry kind she had been wearing when he first met her, tickets for every new musical that came on . . .

Old Joe had sounded a warning. 'You've got an expensive item there, son. You ought to put a curb on her, else she'll run you into debt. What's she want all that gear for? To impress the neighbours?'

That of course had been while the business was still in the old man's hands and was a prosperous concern. Later, when he and Amelia had departed to sunnier shores, it was much less capable of carrying the burden of a spendthrift woman's expenses; especially when the loss of trade was taken into account. They had had no children; and he was thankful now that they had not; though at one time he would have been happy to start a family. But Martine had been dead set against the idea.

'Babies are such a drag. Messy little things too. I don't know how people put up with them. But I suppose it's all a question of taste. And I don't happen to have that particular taste.'

It seemed an odd way for a woman to talk, Caley thought. But he guessed that one powerful reason why she was reluctant to have a child was that she was fearful of losing

14

her figure. She would certainly not have liked that; for if there was one thing she was not lacking in, it was vanity.

So there had been no patter of tiny feet in that household, and now there was only one pair of the adult variety to make a sound in the place. Which he had to admit was rather depressing.

He stubbed out the cigarette and lit another one. He really would have to cut out the smoking. It was far too expensive, and bad for the health too. All the best arguments were against the habit, so he surely must take a grip on himself and give it up.

But not yet. Not until he had finished the packet.

3

Lunch with Chuck

'You're late,' Brogan said. He sounded peevish.

One might have thought, Caley reflected, that after all that time spent in prison he would have learned to be patient. But maybe it worked the other way; maybe an ex-con felt the need to make up for what he had lost.

'I had to find a place to park,' Caley said.

He had had a choice between driving in from Canning Town in the pick-up truck or using public transport, and he had decided that the truck might be the lesser of two evils. He had allowed himself what he thought would be plenty of time, but there was never time enough in the London traffic. It moved at a snail's pace.

Brogan was sitting at a corner table, and if he had not waved a hand Caley might have had difficulty in recognising him. It had been a long time since the two of them had last met, and that time had not dealt kindly with the man. It could hardly have been expected to when so much of it had been spent behind bars.

In fact Brogan had never had much going for him in the way of masculine good looks. Unlike Caley, he was not just ordinary. Indeed, some people would have said he was downright ugly. There had been a time when he had had some pretensions to becoming a top rank professional boxer, but he had never had the talent, and all that prizefighting had done for him was to knock his face into rather worse shape than it had been before and endow it with some unsightly scar tissue above the eyebrows. Now there was a pallid flabbiness about his features that had not been there when Caley had last seen him.

The restaurant was pretty full and there was the usual buzz of conversation mingling with the clinking of tableware. Brogan was wearing a blue suit that looked a trifle out of fashion. It also had creases in the wrong places, as though it had been folded up and stowed away for quite a time.

Something about Brogan that struck Caley immediately was that the man was nervous. He kept glancing here and there, as though half expecting to see someone he would rather not have seen among the other customers. Now and then he would cast his eye in the direction of the entrance, possibly to see who was coming in. He was certainly on edge, and Caley wondered why. Perhaps this was one of the ways a spell in prison affected you — or at least affected him. It could be that he had enemies on the outside; people he preferred not to meet.

It did not however affect his appetite. He ordered grilled beef-steak with roast potatoes and all the trimmings, and he ate like a hog. That too might have been a habit acquired in prison. Or maybe he had always eaten like that. Caley could not remember.

Conversation was desultory. After so many years without any contact between the two of them it might have been supposed that there would have been no end of things to talk about. But it was not like that at all; for much of the time they both seemed strangely tongue-tied.

There was of course one subject which would have been of great interest to Caley: the little matter of a bullion raid, for the participation in which Brogan had been for a length of time deprived of his liberty. But, perhaps not unnaturally, friend Chuck showed no inclination to touch on that matter; and for his part Caley felt it would hardly have been at all tactful to mention it.

So the meal progressed with nothing of any great interest having been said, and certainly no mention of that something that was to be of advantage to him which Brogan had hinted at on the telephone. Maybe it had just been a piece of bait to persuade him to accept the luncheon invitation. But why anyway should the man have been so keen on a meeting if, as now seemed likely, he had nothing of any importance to say?

They had reached the coffee stage when Brogan appeared to come to a decision. He dipped a hand into his breast pocket and pulled out a small sealed envelope, buff-coloured. He kept it covered with his hand as he passed it across the table, making the whole action appear somewhat furtive.

'I'd like you to keep this for me,' he said.

'What is it?' Caley asked.

There appeared to be no marking on the envelope to give a clue to what might be inside it.

'Never mind what it is,' Brogan said. 'Put it in your pocket.' He was glancing around as if to see whether anyone at another table might have observed what was going on. 'Quick now.'

Caley was aware of the urgency in his voice and he did what was asked.

'Now are you going to tell me what all this is about?'

Brogan hesitated, seemed about to say something, then changed his mind and was silent.

'Ah, come on,' Caley said. 'You've got to tell me what this is all about. Am I to open the envelope?'

Brogan answered hastily: 'No, don't do that. I just want you to keep it until I ask you to give it back.'

'But that doesn't make sense.'

'To me it does.'

'Now tell me,' Caley said. 'Could this have anything to do with what you were talking about on the phone? Something to my advantage is what you said.'

'Could be. Could be just that.'

'But you're not going to tell me what it is right now?'

'No. It'll keep. There's no hurry.'

It sounded ridiculous to Caley. It seemed obvious to him that Brogan had some bee in his bonnet, but what it was he would have to wait to find out. Maybe all that time spent behind bars had turned the man's head. Maybe he was just plain gaga. But Caley doubted that. There was surely some purpose behind it all, which for some reason or other he hesitated to reveal.

A little later Caley paid a visit to the toilet, and when he came back he saw at once that the situation had altered. Brogan was no longer alone at the table. There were two men with him.

One of the men was on Brogan's left and the other on his right. It was as though they were hemming him in, and he was looking nervous to say the least. Indeed, one might have said that he was looking decidedly scared. And when Caley had taken a look at the two newcomers he could not help reflecting that they were the kind who might scare anyone of a timid disposition; and maybe a lot of others besides.

The one on Brogan's right was thin, almost to the point of emaciation. He had greasy black hair which could have used the attentions of a barber, and his cheeks were so hollow that the bones above them jutted out like twin knobs. He had a hooked nose, which gave him something of the look of a bird of prey. And indeed there was altogether a predatory look about him, as though he were ready to snap up anything of value that might come within his range. He was certainly not the kind of character it would have been a pleasure to meet in a deserted alleyway late at night. Or at any other time for that matter.

The other one was a contrast: podgy, round-faced, shaven-headed. He looked less dangerous than the thin man, but this might have been misleading; one could not always judge accurately by appearance. Anyway, it was evident that Brogan was feeling very ill-at-ease in the presence of these two individuals who had planted themselves, apparently uninvited, at his table. They had certainly not been on his guest list although he appeared to be well acquainted with them.

Caley had come to a halt. There was a large shrub in a container which afforded him partial concealment from the table, and none of the three seated there appeared to have noticed him.

The men were keeping their voices low and he could not catch what they were saying, but he could guess by their gestures and expressions that they were pretty annoyed about something and were giving Brogan a hard time. He on his part was saying little and was looking more and more like a trapped animal, searching for a way out. But they had him cornered and they knew it. He could not simply get up and walk away.

Then it happened; and it was so completely unexpected. For it was not the lean-faced one with the predatory look who lost control. It was the podgy one with the round face and the bullet-head, the seemingly less likely of the two to resort to physical violence, who did so. In fact it looked as though the other was trying to restrain him, but to no avail.

'Oh to hell with this,' the podgy one said. 'We're getting nowhere with the bugger and

I've had enough of him.'

He shoved his chair back, stood up and got himself behind Brogan before the other one could stop him.

Brogan started to get up as well, but he was too late. The podgy man hauled a small pistol from his pocket and shot him in the back of the head.

4

Dead Man

Caley was petrified. It was so unexpected and so brutal. He had an impulse to start running, to get away from that scene without delay. But he did not move.

Brogan had slumped forward onto the table with his nose in a coffee cup; blood and brains spattered on the cloth, dead as the steak he had consumed such a short while earlier.

The two men had vanished. One moment they were there and the next moment they had gone. Perhaps they had suddenly remembered a pressing engagement elsewhere.

A woman was screaming. There was hubbub at the tables near to Brogan's. In other parts of the restaurant with no clear view of the shot man people were asking one another what had happened. Waiters had come to a halt with dishes in their hands, not knowing what to do.

The manager appeared from somewhere. It was a woman; large, ginger-haired, competent.

'My God!' she said. 'What happened?'

One of the waiters told her. 'Two men

came in, sat down at that table. One of them shot him.'

'You saw it?'

'No. I heard the shot, saw the men heading for the door.'

'So they've gone?'

'Oh, they've gone all right. Wouldn't expect them to hang around, would you?'

'But this is terrible, terrible. Was there anyone else with the — er — ' She seemed to hesitate to say 'the dead man', though it was evident that Brogan was never going to move around again of his own volition.

'Yes, there was,' the waiter said. And suddenly he noticed Caley hovering nearby and trying to look inconspicuous. 'Why you, sir. You were with him, weren't you?'

Caley had no choice but to step forward and admit the fact, since the waiter was the one who had served that table.

'Well, yes, I was with him. His name's Brogan. But I wasn't here when the other men came in. I'd gone to the toilet. I'd only just got back when the shooting took place.'

The woman gave him a hard look, as if she found this difficult to believe. Then she said: 'I shall have to call the police and an ambulance. Don't go away.'

Caley had no intention of going away. He

had lost the chance. He was just wishing he had never accepted Brogan's invitation to lunch. He might have guessed it would turn out badly. But not surely as badly as this. He thought of all the repercussions there would be for him. He could not avoid being involved. He had been having lunch with a known criminal, a recently discharged jail-bird who in the course of the meal had got himself shot in the head. There were plenty of people who would regard that as highly suspicious. And among those people would undoubtedly be the police.

As if he needed more troubles!

The shooting had, not surprisingly, upset the orderly routine of the restaurant. It could hardly have been expected to function normally when there was a dead body at one of the tables. It was as upsetting as Banquo's ghost at Macbeth's banquet.

Nevertheless, some hardy souls had resumed eating; though these tended to be those who were furthest away from the late Chuck Brogan. Some were even ordering second courses when they could manage to get the attention of a waiter. Others appeared to have slipped unobtrusively away, possibly without paying. All in all, the smooth running of the Top Notch had been thrown completely out of gear by the unfortunate and totally unforeseen incident at the table in the corner.

* * *

The police were the first to arrive: two uniformed constables in a patrol car, quickly followed by a detective sergeant and a constable in plain clothes. An ambulance appeared shortly afterwards, but there was nothing the two attendants could do for Brogan; he was past human aid. However, it was left to the medico who got to the Top Notch rather later to confirm what was obvious to anyone with eyes in his head, that Chuck Brogan was indeed dead.

Caley had at once been pointed out by the waiter who had served him and Brogan as the one who had been lunching with the dead man. He could not deny it, and the detective sergeant was the first to start questioning him.

'Your name, sir?'

Caley told him.

'And the other — er — gentleman?'

The last word seemed to stick in his throat. Brogan had hardly looked like a gentleman when he had been alive. Dead and in his present inelegant posture he looked even less like one.

'His name,' Caley said, 'is Brogan, Chuck Brogan. At least that's what people called him. Actually he was Herbert Arthur.'

The sergeant noted this down. He was still questioning Caley when the detective chief inspector arrived and it all had to be gone over again. The name Chuck Brogan had not appeared to touch any chord with the sergeant, but the chief inspector, whose name was Cartwright, had a better memory.

'Chuck Brogan! So they let him out.'

'Yes,' Caley said.

'Didn't do him much good, did it? He'd have been safer on the inside.'

Cartwright was a tall, skinny man with a stoop. He was maybe getting on for forty and gave the impression of being the kind of officer who had seen it all and took nothing on trust. It would have been useless telling a pack of lies to him because he would not have believed you. Lots of criminals had tried it in the past and it had got them nowhere. Cartwright might not have believed the truth either, but that was another matter.

'And you were having lunch with him, Mr Caley?'

'Yes.'

'Did you know he was just out?'

'Well yes, but — '

'But still you didn't mind sharing a table with him?'

'He was very pressing.'

'So it was his idea?'

'Yes. He rang me up.'

'When was the arrangement made?'

'Yesterday.'

'Did he give any particular reason why he wanted to meet you?'

Caley decided not to mention the hint Brogan had given that it might be to his advantage. Instinct warned him that this might not count in his favour with the chief inspector.

So he answered: 'No, he didn't.'

Cartwright's eyes scanned Caley's face, and he felt uneasy under the scrutiny. It was as though the eyes, which were a kind of steely grey, were probing his mind and discovering all sorts of hidden secrets; guilty ones at that.

'Can you think of any reason?'

'Well, we were at school together. Sort of pals at one time, I suppose you might say.'

'Ah!'

Caley did not care for that 'Ah!' It suggested to him that Cartwright was reading all sorts of things in that admission. So he hastened to add: 'But that was a long time ago. We haven't had anything to do with each other for years.'

'No, you wouldn't, would you?' The chief inspector spoke drily. 'Seeing where he's been of late. You didn't visit him?'

'No, never.'

'And yet you're the one he picks to have lunch with as soon as he's out. Doesn't that seem a little strange to you?'

'Not really. I don't suppose he could think of anyone else.' Cartwright's thin lips emitted a sound rather like 'Humph!' It seemed to indicate a certain doubt regarding this simple explanation. Caley was uncomfortably conscious of the envelope in his pocket. He felt as though those probing eyes of the chief inspector might have a kind of X-ray quality, enabling them to see through the fabric of the jacket and discover that incriminating piece of evidence.

Yet why should it be incriminating? It was just a plain buff envelope, sealed but with no inscription on it. There was nothing to indicate that Brogan had given it to him even if they searched him. And could they legally do that? Just because he had been having lunch with the dead man? Would it be within the law? Surely not. Nevertheless, he felt a vague sense of guilt for not having mentioned this piece of paper that Brogan had handed to him with no information regarding what was inside the envelope or why he wanted Caley to keep it for him.

It was a mystery, and it was one he felt sure Cartwright would have been interested in. But he was damned if he would tell the man about it. Why should he? There was a stubborn streak in Caley when it came to the push and it overrode his qualms regarding the concealment from the police of anything that might have a bearing on the case.

Moreover, there was that hint of something to his advantage which Brogan had given. Suppose the envelope had something to do with that, and he lost out by handing it over to the forces of law and order. He could not for the present imagine just how he might stand to benefit from it, but perhaps all would be revealed when he opened the envelope. As he fully intended doing at the first opportunity now that Chuck was dead and could have no further interest in it.

More police officers had arrived and were taking statements from those customers who had not made a quick getaway. One was searching for fingerprints at the table where the crime had taken place, and Cartwright told Caley that they would need his for elimination purposes. He said these could be taken at the station, and Caley realised then that he would not be allowed to go straight home. He supposed it was hardly to be expected that he would.

'At least,' Cartwright said, 'you had your lunch.' And his lips twitched minimally in what could almost have been a smile.

It occurred to Caley that it was a lunch for two that had not been paid for, and the thought came to him that he might be expected to foot the bill. But nobody had mentioned that little matter and he was certainly not going to bring up the subject.

Business in the restaurant had of necessity come to a halt. Nothing was being served and later customers arriving at the door were turned away. They would have to seek their luncheons elsewhere. There was nothing like a dead man at one of the tables and police crawling all over the place to put a damper on the catering.

Caley hung around. When his legs began to ache he managed to get a chair and sit down. Detective Chief Inspector Cartwright had drifted away and he felt abandoned. He wanted a cigarette, and he took out a packet and had got one halfway to his lips when it occurred to him that perhaps smoking would not be in order and he put it away again.

It seemed an age before Cartwright came back and spoke to him.

'Right then,' he said. 'Let's go.'

5

Interrogation

Caley rode to the police station in the back of Cartwright's car with a constable driving. The chief inspector told him that he could pick up his truck later.

'We won't be keeping you long.'

It turned out to be longer than Caley expected. He could not remember when he had last been inside a police station. He was not sure he had ever been in one. He had seen a lot of them on television. You could hardly ever switch your set on without seeing coppers doing their stuff. But none of the TV stations bore much resemblance to the one he was taken to.

They took his fingerprints; which was a messy business and made him feel more and more like a criminal. And then it was the interrogation all over again; this time in what he believed was called an interview room.

Cartwright and the detective sergeant, whose name turned out to be Brown, were the interviewers, and he got the impression that they were not entirely satisfied with his answers. They appeared to suspect that he knew a good deal more than he was admitting.

Like the identity of the killer and his companion.

'You are sure you don't know who they were?'

'Yes. I told you that.'

'You'd never seen them before?'

'Never.'

'Yet you knew Chuck Brogan.'

'Of course. Why else would he have invited me to lunch with him?'

'And you didn't mind lunching with a convicted criminal?'

Caley decided to skip that one this time round.

'You knew of course he was involved in a bullion robbery and served a prison sentence for his part in it?'

'Yes. But he pleaded innocent, didn't he?'

'Just so,' Cartwright said. 'And that's where he made his big mistake.'

'Mistake?'

'Yes. If he had pleaded guilty, told where he'd hidden the gold and named his accomplices he'd have got off with a lighter sentence.'

'But if he really was innocent and had nothing to do with the robbery — '

Both policemen gave a laugh at this. A rather sneering one.

'If you believe that,' Cartwright said, 'you'll believe anything. You being an old pal of his, you ought to know him better.'

Caley denied the relationship. 'We were never pals.'

'You said you were.'

'Well it wasn't really as close as that. Frankly, I never liked the man. Nobody did.'

'So how come you were the one he invited to have lunch with him?'

'I suppose there was nobody else he could think of. Like I said, we were at school together.' He wondered why Cartwright would keep harping on this question, which he had answered before. 'In those days he sort of pushed himself on me. He wasn't popular, you see. No one else would have anything to do with him.'

'But you did?'

'I couldn't avoid him. He battened on to me.'

Caley was recalling how it had been all those years ago. He had been a bit of an outsider himself, and Brogan maybe saw in him a kindred soul. And now Caley remembered also that Brogan had always been a liar and a cheat; so it was really no wonder that he had gone off the rails later in life.

'Tell me,' Cartwright said. 'What did you talk about?'

'Oh, this and that.'

'He didn't mention the little matter of a bullion robbery?'

'No. I told you.'

'Didn't, for instance, say where he'd hidden the loot?'

'Now why would he have told me that, even if he had done it? Which we still don't know, do we?'

They both gave another laugh at that. The suggestion that Brogan might have been innocent really did seem to amuse them.

Caley had a sense of guilt that made him uneasy under the interrogation. He could not forget the envelope in his pocket which Brogan had given him. Somehow he felt it must have a connection with the robbery and that he was maybe withholding vital information. Which was a punishable offence, was it not?

And then there was the matter of his fingerprints. He had heard that when they were taken simply for purposes of elimination of an innocent party they were destroyed afterwards. But no one at the station had mentioned this to him, and he had a nasty feeling that his would be kept on file so that they would be there for possible future reference. Just as if he were a real criminal.

He tried to convince himself that all this was ridiculous, since he was simply there to help the police with their enquiries. But it was no use; the feeling persisted.

'When did you last see Chuck Brogan?' Cartwright asked. 'Before today, that is.'

'Oh, years ago.'

'How many years?'

'I can't say exactly. After leaving school we rather lost touch. We may have met by chance once or twice. I can't really remember.'

The truth was that he had done his best to avoid Brogan. Especially when he began to hear rumours that friend Chuck was getting himself mixed up in somewhat criminal activities. He could not remember who had told him this, but it was of no consequence.

'And you didn't visit him in prison?'

'No. Why would I have done that?'

'Old pals.'

'Like I told you, we were never that close. I don't even know what prison he was in.'

'So,' Cartwright said, 'let's get this straight. You had lunch with Brogan at his invitation, and all through the meal he never mentioned the small matter of a gold bullion heist in which he was involved. Is that it?'

Caley thought they had had this straight already. He wished the two policemen would not keep repeating the questions.

'We still don't know he was involved. It might have been a miscarriage of justice.'

This time instead of laughing they just looked pained.

'And you didn't recognise either of the two men who came to the table while you were away?'

This was another of the questions he had already answered. He suspected that they were trying to catch him out. Asking the same questions again and again; first Cartwright and then Brown; a double act.

But the answer was still the same. 'I'd never seen them before.'

'Describe them.'

'But I've done that.'

'Do it again. You may think of something you've left out.'

So he did it again, as best he could. Which he had to admit was not very good.

'Well, as I said, one was thin and bony in the face. He had black hair, rather long. The other one, the one who shot Brogan, was shorter, rather fat, head shaved.'

'What were they wearing?'

'Leather jackets and jeans, I think. Oh, and black gloves. Thin leather, I'd say.'

'Gloves!' Cartwright said. 'Hell and damnation! Why didn't you tell us that before?'

'I forgot.'

'So much for the dabs,' Brown said, 'Smart boys.'

★ ★ ★

They took Caley's address before letting him go. He felt he was really in their hands now, and he did not like it. He had never previously had anything to do with the police, and if Brogan had not pressed him to accept the invitation to lunch he would still have had none. And still everything would have been fine if two hard characters had not walked in and left Chuck with his cranium ruined and his nose in a coffee cup.

He wondered who they were and why they had been so mad at Brogan. Though of course he had been the kind of man who might have made anyone mad. And those two must have known him long ago, before he went behind bars. They had obviously had a great desire to talk to him about something and they had been pretty clever in tracing him to the Top Notch.

He doubted whether they had had any intention of killing him. But the podgy one had lost his temper and the deed had been done before the other one could stop him. Which meant that they had not got what they had come for. And then it occurred to him to wonder whether that small envelope now resting in his pocket could have had some bearing on the visit. It made him uneasy just to think about this possibility. He wondered precisely what he had got himself involved in. Something dangerous, that was for sure. And he did not like danger; it frightened him. But he could see no way out of it now.

★ ★ ★

A constable in a police car took him back to where he had left his pick-up truck. There was a parking-ticket attached to the windscreen.

It was just what he needed to complete his day.

6

Puzzle

It was growing dusk when he reached home. The evenings were beginning to have an autumnal air in these last days of summer, and daylight was fading early on a day as dull as this one, with a drizzle of rain beginning to fall.

Caley parked his truck in the yard and went into his office and switched on the light. As a precaution he lowered the blind. There was no one outside who might have peeped through the window, but he felt the need for privacy and he was taking no chances.

He took the envelope that Brogan had given him from his pocket and laid it on the desk. He did not open it at once; he sat on a chair at the desk and lit a cigarette. He stared at the envelope while he smoked as if mesmerised by it. Brogan had told him not to open it, but he was gone and would never be coming back, so the prohibition was no longer valid.

Nevertheless, when he had smoked the cigarette down to the butt and had taken up a paper-knife he still hesitated to slit the envelope open. And when he finally did so he could not avoid a certain feeling of guilt, as though he had carried out a nefarious deed.

It was therefore something of an anticlimax when he extracted the contents of the small buff envelope.

There was nothing inside but a scrap of paper which might have been torn from a cheap jotting pad. It had the appearance of having been in somebody's pocket for quite a while. It was a trifle frayed at the edges and was certainly grubby.

Caley stared at it and had a sense of disappointment; of having been cheated even. He could hardly have said what he had been expecting: a message of some kind perhaps, maybe giving some clue as to why Brogan had been so insistent that he should take especial care of it. But there was no message, no writing of any kind except for a few block letters scattered here and there.

Besides the letters there were some straggling lines meandering across the paper and joining up in three places to form a rough triangle.

At a few places along the lines, where the letters were, some little squares were jumbled together like boxes. In another place just outside the triangle were three parallel marks rather like arrows, with a cross near their base and the letters SB at their points. The markings had all been made by a soft pencil and were rather faint but still legible.

Caley could make no sense of the thing, and he wondered whether Brogan had been playing some elaborate game with him. But he dismissed this idea at once; the man had been dead serious when he had confided the envelope to his old acquaintance with strict instructions not to open it. So obviously this scrap of paper lying on the desk had been of great importance to him. But for the life of him Caley could not fathom out why. To him it conveyed no message and made no sense whatever. Yet Brogan, under pressure, had admitted that the contents of the envelope could have some bearing on the hint he had given that he had something to confide which might be to Caley's advantage. And of course he had never got round to revealing what he had meant by this statement. And never would now, unfortunately.

It was a puzzle; and Caley had never been much of a hand at solving puzzles. The Daily Telegraph crossword was far beyond his ability at that kind of thing. So however much he might stare at this crude drawing that Brogan presumably had made, he could not find the slightest meaning in it.

He took another cigarette from the packet and discovered that it was the last one. He debated with himself whether to light it at once or leave it until later. He decided to smoke it and then go out and buy some more; because he was really hooked on the weed again, and what with all the problems now facing him he felt he could not manage without it.

When he had smoked the cigarette down to the butt he was no nearer discovering any meaning in the slip of paper that Brogan had given him. Yet the man must have put some value on it; possibly a great deal of value; even adding up to a horde of gold? Now there was a thought.

But then he had got himself killed without revealing why this should have been so. Well of course he could hardly be blamed for that. He had not asked to be killed, though it was pretty obvious that he had done something to make those two men mad at him; so mad that one of them had been sufficiently steamed up to lose control of himself and come out with the old equaliser and plant a slug in Brogan's head.

A likely deduction was that they had been trying to extract some information from him, and that he had been stubbornly refusing to divulge it. So was this information in some way connected with the grubby little piece of paper now lying on his desk? This seemed fairly likely; and for some reason or other it had to be of considerable value.

But still Caley could think of no possible answer to the riddle that confronted him. So eventually he decided to give up racking his brains for the present and go out and buy some of those cigarettes for which his body was craving.

Before leaving the office, however, he took the precaution of locking the paper in an old iron safe which stood in one corner of the room. Not that he expected anyone was likely to break into the house and purloin the article while he was gone; a burglar would surely turn his attention to a more prosperous-looking establishment. Nevertheless, it was advisable not to take any risks. The sketch might look valueless, but Brogan had obviously set considerable store by it, and he certainly knew something concerning it which he had been unwilling to reveal to Caley at that time. And now of course he never would reveal it, unless he reappeared as a ghost and started spilling the beans; which to Caley appeared somewhat unlikely.

★ ★ ★

There was a public house named The Coach and Horses not far from Caley's place, and it was to this establishment that he went for his cigarettes. And while he was there he decided to have a drink. It was early evening and the bar was filling up. There was the usual hum of conversation, and he wondered how many of the customers were talking about the shooting at the Top Notch. The news of it would surely have got into the evening papers and would have been on the air. He just hoped his name would not have been revealed, but he could not be sure of that. Would he be notorious now as a man who had lunched with a criminal, an ex-convict, who had been shot in the head by one of a pair of hoodlums while he, Caley, had temporarily left the table? Maybe. And notoriety was the last thing he wanted at that time.

He was not a regular at The Coach and Horses, and he could see no one there with whom he was acquainted; which was a relief.

He went to the bar and ordered a double scotch as well as the cigarettes and was shocked by the price of it. It was not a drink he often bought; in fact he could not remember when he had last tasted the stuff. He was far from being a regular boozer, but he had felt the need on this occasion of something a good deal stronger than tea or coffee after the ordeal of the afternoon.

He withdrew to a seat in a corner after paying what was due, but he had hardly had time to take a mouthful of the whisky and light a cigarette when he was accosted by a little whippet of a man in patched jeans and a dirty sweater.

'Why, hello there, Mr Caley. Don't often see you in 'ere.'

'I don't often come here,' Caley said.

He knew the man simply because he had been an occasional customer. His name was Ogden, and he was in a small way of business as a painter and decorator. He had been in the habit of calling now and then in his white van at the Caley yard for paint and other supplies. Caley had never liked him; Ogden was a know-all of a particularly offensive type in Caley's opinion, and he was not at all pleased to encounter him now when he would much rather have been allowed to drink his whisky and smoke his cigarette in peace.

Ogden of course was having none of that. There was a space on the seat next to Caley and he slipped into it, pint mug of brown ale in hand.

'Jew 'ear about that there shooting in a restaurant earlier in the day, Mr C?'

For a moment Caley suspected that Ogden was teasing him, knowing full well that he had been involved. But then he realised that some of the details, including the name of the person who had been taking lunch with the victim, had not yet been revealed to the general public.

'Yes, I heard about it.'

'You ask me, it was a bit of gang warfare. Things is getting bad again, like when the Krays and Richardsons was at it. It's them there Chinks and Jamaican Yardies now. Oughter kick 'em all out, I say. Clean the place up for us as belong 'ere.'

'I don't think there were any of them involved.'

'Maybe not. But there could've been. What we need is more bobbies on the beat. Arrest the buggers, I say.'

Caley wondered which buggers Ogden was referring to. But he did not ask; he just wished the man would go away. But there seemed to be no hope of that. Ogden had a listener and did not intend to let him go.

'It's all about these here drugs, you know. Junkies everywhere you look. Gotta 'ave their fix. Take to crime to get the cash to pay for the stuff. Heroin, crack, you name it. I dunno what the country's coming to. Bloody rack and ruin, I shouldn't wonder. Now take this 'ere euro business — '

Caley decided not to take it. He drained his glass and stood up. 'I have to go. Got an appointment.'

Ogden nodded. 'Business, is it?'

'Sort of.'

'Heard about your bit of trouble. Too bad. Where'll I get my stuff now?'

Caley neither knew nor cared. He had bigger worries than Ogden's. If he had been an employee made redundant by some large firm along with a few hundred others he would simply have gone on the dole and looked for another job. It was different when you had been self-employed and your business went down the drain. Everything became more complicated. You had no trade and no experience of working for somebody else. When he was younger, of course, his father had employed him; but that was not quite the same thing; it was all in the family and he had known that eventually the business would be his.

When he had first realised that things were getting really bad and that he had the choice of closing down and rescuing what he could from the wreck or carrying on until overtaken by bankruptcy he had felt physically sick. Frightened too. He just did not know what to do. He wished there had been someone to

49

help him, to advise; but there had been no one. He was on his own.

And of course Martine had walked out on him. It was only to be expected; a rat leaving the sinking ship. But she would have been no help to him even if she had stayed. He was better off without her nagging at him.

What a fool he had been to marry her! He could hardly have found anyone less suited to be his wife. Old Joe had seen through her from the start of course; seen the shallowness of her. He realised that now. But his father had been guarded in his comments; he could hardly have stated openly that the marriage would be a disaster, even though he might think so. And so it had ended like this.

'People like us,' Ogden said, 'we 'ave a 'ard time of it these days. We ain't big enough, that's what it is. We're little people, that's what. We get trampled on by the big business lot.' He gave a sniff. 'Still, we gotta do what we can, even if it ain't much use. I wish you luck, Mr C. Reckon you'll need it.'

And that, Caley reflected, was probably his way of cheering you up.

7

Gloom

The name of the lean hawkfaced man was Josh Tulley. The short, fatter character, the one who had done the killing, was known as Slim Harker. There was a third man with them, and the three were in conference.

This conference was taking place at a dilapidated old house in the East End that was one of a row earmarked for demolition. Most of these were already unoccupied, their windows broken by stone-throwing urchins. The discussion had tended at times to become a trifle heated, even a touch recriminatory. The target for this recrimination was of course Slim Harker, who was accused by the other two of being a trigger-happy bastard who had probably wrecked their entire operation.

The third man, whose name was Harold Starke and who was known for obvious reasons as Lugs, was particularly vituperative.

'Beats me how anybody could be so plain bloody stupid. Without Chuck we're back to square one. Why'd you have to go and shoot him?'

Starke was the only one of the three who was dressed in a suit. Apart from the protruding ears, he was not a bad-looking man. He was coming up to thirty-five years old, and when not on a job was usually well turned out. Unfortunately, at the present time money was particularly hard to come by and his one remaining suit was showing unmistakable signs of wear and tear.

Women were attracted to him; they thought he looked nice. Really there was nothing nice about him; he was as nasty as they came; a rat of the first water. Like the other two, he was known to the police; but for the present, to their regret, they had nothing they could pin on any of them.

Harker repeated the excuse he had already made. 'It was the spur of the moment. He really got my goat, telling us he didn't know where the gold was. If he didn't know, who did, for God's sake?'

'Well, sure he knew, but putting a slug in his noggin was no way to get the info out of him.'

'I know, I know. And I'm sorry.'

'Sorry! Is that all you can say?'

'What else do you want me to say? You asking me to go down on my knees and beg forgiveness?'

'You tryin' to be funny?'

'Do I look like I'm bein' funny?'

'No. You look like a bastard what's buggered things up for all of us. We oughter string you up, that's what.'

Tulley put his spoke in then. 'Now hold it. This ain't gettin' us nowhere. Thing's done and that's all there is to it. Now we gotta do some thinking.'

'Take more than thinking to get our pugs on the yellow stuff,' Starke said. But he was beginning to cool down.

They were all sitting at a rough deal table in a dingy kitchen with a grimy window looking out onto a small wall-enclosed backyard. There were beer cans on the table, some full, some empty. All three men were smoking and there were cigarette butts on the floor.

'He wasn't going to tell us anyway,' Harker said.

Starke sneered. 'Well, you sure made certain he never got the chance to change his mind.'

It had not been skilful tracking that had led Tulley and Harker to the Top Notch, where Brogan was lunching with Caley. It had in fact been sheer luck. Harold Starke had spotted Brogan coming out of a shop and had followed him. He had seen him enter the restaurant and had immediately got in touch with Tulley on his mobile phone. Tulley had been at the house with Harker, and the two of them had lost no time in heading for the Top Notch in Tulley's car, a rather old Renault which was in their straitened condition the only one they now possessed.

Because of a traffic jam it had taken them quite a while to reach the restaurant, and they were afraid they would find the bird flown; but as things turned out they arrived just at the end of the meal when Caley had gone to the toilet. It could not have been better timing. The only snag was that Brogan had refused to talk.

'The bastard was holding out on us,' Starke said. 'I wonder why.'

'Well,' Tulley said, 'maybe he figured that as he'd been the one that done the porridge he was entitled to the reward.'

'That would be greedy, wouldn't it?'

'Maybe not to his way of thinking.'

'This other guy,' Harker said. 'The one he was having a meal with. Where does he fit in?'

They thought about that for a while, smoking and drinking as if to spur their brains to action.

Finally Starke said: 'You reckon he told the bloke where the gold was hid?'

'Why would he do that?' Tulley said.

'Well, look at it this way. The filth are going

to keep a pretty sharp eye on him, so he won't dare go near where it's hid. But somebody else might.'

'He'd need to be paid, this other guy.'

'Of course he would. But it'd have been worth it to Chuck even if it cost him a bar of the stuff.'

'You think he'd have trusted anybody that much?'

'Depends on the man. An old buddie maybe.'

'Well,' Harker said, 'it'd have to be a real close buddie, and he'd have to be bent an' all. Else he might be shouting copper at the top of his voice soon's he heard what Chuck was proposing.'

'But he didn't, did he?'

'That's true.'

'So,' Tulley said, 'did he tell the guy anything or didn't he? That's the question.'

Starke gave a laugh. He seemed to be getting over his bad humour and accepting the situation as it was.

'One way of finding out.'

'Which is?'

'We go and ask him.'

'But not yet,' Tulley said.

'Why not?'

'Because the coppers could be thinking along the same lines as us. And if he's holding out on them they'll not be letting him out of their sight. We've gotta watch our step. Besides, we don't know where he hangs out.'

'We can find him.'

'Sure we can. In time. But there's no need to rush things. We've waited a long time, so why lose patience now?'

'I bet it seemed a hell of a lot longer to Chuck,' Harker said. 'He musta bin thinking all the time of what was waiting for him when he got out.'

'And then all he had was a slug in the brainbox,' Starke said. And he gave Harker a long hard look.

'Lay off it,' Harker said. 'We've been through all that and it gets us nowhere.'

It was growing dark outside. Tulley stood up, switched the light on and drew a ragged curtain across the window. There was no one in the yard to look in, but they valued privacy and took no risks of being spied upon. They had plenty to hide.

'Where you think he stashed it?' Starke said.

'In the ground somewhere for sure,' Tulley said.

'Seems likely. He had a spade in the van and it wasn't there when the police searched it, by all accounts.'

'Musta dropped it off somewhere afore

they caught up with him.'

'And no doubt a long way from where he did the digging.'

'In a ditch maybe.'

'Well, it makes no difference now. We can take it that the stuff's buried and nobody's yet found it. It'd've been in the news if they had.'

'Smart boy, our Chuck,' Tulley said.

'A sight smarter than some,' Starke said. And he shot another sharp glance at Harker, which said it all.

'There's one good thing you can say about old Chuck — he never blew the gaff on us. Coulda done hisself a bit of good with the judge if he had.'

'You think that was for our sakes? Not on your Nellie. He was looking out for number one. Meant to have the lot when he came out. All for hisself.'

'Maybe you're right. We'll never know now.'

There was a shared feeling of depression in that dingy kitchen. They had all been waiting with expectation for Brogan's release, feeling certain that they would be able to shake the information they needed out of him. If they had known just when he was coming out they would have been waiting at the prison entrance. But they had not possessed that vital information and it had only been

Starke's unexpected sighting of him that had put them on his tail. It had been their big break; and then because of his obstinacy and Harker's loss of patience, it had all turned sour. Now they had only Caley to work on, with the added complication of the police looking for Brogan's killer, who just happened to be sitting at the table with the other two.

They had all known the inside of a prison at one time or another, but not for any long term. Essentially they were small-time criminals. The bullion heist had been an exception for them; a move up the scale. The information regarding the shipment had come to them fortuitously: a man, having had rather too much to drink in a public house, had confided to them what he should have kept to himself.

This man, Draper, was a security guard. He was perhaps as greedy as they were and willing to be corrupted. It was their big chance. Maybe it was what they had been waiting for throughout all those years of petty crime. Now they could all become rich and retire to the Costa Brava, to the Spanish sunshine and the sweet life.

They were short of a wheelman and they roped in Brogan. He had something of a reputation among the criminal fraternity and was available. It was a mistake; they could see that now. And the mistake had been compounded by Harker's loss of temper. Now Harker could be on a murder charge, with the other two as accomplices.

If the Bill got onto them.

As they might.

All in all, there was good reason for the feeling of gloom in that wretched kitchen.

8

If Anything

'He's lying, of course,' Cartwright said.

Detective Sergeant William Brown glanced at him enquiringly. 'Who, sir?'

'Caley, of course. Who else?'

'You think so?'

'I'm damned certain of it. He knows a sight more than he's letting on. That was more than just a friendly get-together between him and Brogan. There was more behind it than that.'

'Yes, I'd say there was,' Brown said. 'But what?'

They were in Cartwright's office which was a pretty spartan room furnished with a desk, three chairs, a filing cabinet and a coatstand. The detective chief inspector was seated at the desk with his back to a window looking out onto a forecourt where some police cars were parked. It was raining and water was dripping from two plane trees in the background. Beyond the trees traffic could be seen passing along a road. It was not the kind of view calculated to give much of a lift to the spirits.

'Now that's the question, isn't it?' Cartwright said.

'You think it might have had something to do with the gold?'

'Frankly I can't see any other reason why Brogan would have wanted to give Caley a free lunch.'

'Old pals getting together for a natter?'

'He said they were not that close.'

'Well, he would, wouldn't he?'

'True,' Cartwright said. 'Who'd want to be associated with a known criminal?'

'So what are you suggesting Brogan told him?'

'Maybe where he stashed the gold.'

'For what reason?'

'For the reason that he wanted somebody neutral to pick the stuff up for him. Knowing he himself would be a marked man for a long time to come.'

It was the same conclusion that three other men had come to rather earlier. It had to be the obvious one.

'So,' Brown said, 'your guess is that this Caley character is bent?'

'As a corkscrew. Even if he's been an upright honest citizen for years, this could have been too great a temptation for him to resist. Look at it this way — his wife's left him and his business is going down the drain; so he's in real trouble. Then a chance of getting his fingers on some of the stuff that makes the world go round comes along. In his shoes wouldn't you grab it?'

They had made enquiries regarding Caley's financial situation and it had given Cartwright food for thought. A man in as much trouble as that might snatch at any straw to keep himself afloat. And a slice of gold bullion would have been a pretty substantial straw.

★　★　★

They had hauled Starke, Tulley and Harker in for questioning; not because they had anything solid to pin on them, but simply because they had at one time been linked with the bullion robbery. This had been years ago, but it had never been possible to get enough evidence for a conviction. Besides which the men all had alibis which appeared to stand up. So all three of them had to be allowed to go scot-free.

Cartwright, then a young detective sergeant, had worked on the case and the lack of a successful result, apart from the arrest and sentencing of Brogan, had rankled. He would have loved to get something on the others, and a charge of murder now would have done very well as a starter.

So the three had been rounded up and grilled, but without success. Then Caley had been brought in and there had been three separate identity parades with him looking through the one-way glass and being invited to pick out anyone he remembered as being at his table at the Top Notch on the fatal day. He had recognised Tulley and Harker at once, but each time he had shaken his head.

'Sorry, no.'

He was being wary. He did not wish to be involved. If he put the finger on Harker as the one who had shot Brogan and on Tulley as his accomplice there was no telling what it might lead to. Of course it might see them put away and thus free him from their possible attentions; but then again it might not. And there was always the third man, who was probably just as bad as they were. So, all things considered, it seemed best to be cautious.

Cartwright had been furious. He believed Caley was lying; indeed, he felt sure of it. But he could prove nothing. So, although seething inwardly, he had been forced to contain his anger and let the men go.

Other witnesses proved useless too. Some pointed out one innocent person, some another. Some could not even remember seeing the men. They were all hopeless from Cartwright's point of view, but he had expected little better. Your average person was very unobservant.

★ ★ ★

'If only we could have found the murder weapon,' Brown said, 'we could have pinned it on one of them sure enough. What you think they did with it?'

'Threw it in the Thames most likely,' Cartwright said. 'They may not be tops for brains but they'd have enough savvy not to hold onto the gun.'

'I suppose so. It certainly wasn't in that dump they call home sweet home.'

'What I can never understand is how they ever came to do a bullion heist. It was way out of their league. They're just small-time villains. Robbing corner shops of the money in the till, sub-post offices, that sort of thing. Vicious but not big-time.'

'Maybe they had a hot tip and thought they'd move up in the world. Make a real killing and retire on the proceeds.'

Cartwright shrugged. 'Could be. If so it had to be the night watchman, security guard, call him what you like, who gave the information. But he's kept his trap shut and seems to have faded out of the picture.'

'You think he really lost his memory of everything that happened?'

'Maybe. And again maybe not.'

'But would he keep quiet after what they did to him? They really beat him up. You'd think he'd want to get his own back.'

'Could be scared. Like I said, they're a vicious lot. He may have been afraid he'd get some more of the same if he squealed.'

'True enough,' Brown said, 'But what beats me is why they shot Brogan. If they wanted to get information from him about where he hid the gold they'd have needed to keep him alive. Instead, they just silenced him for good and all.'

'Maybe he'd already given them the info.'

'I doubt it. I think he was holding out on them and one of them lost his temper. Out with the old shooter and bingo, no more Chuck.'

'Tell you one thing,' Cartwright said. 'They must be feeling the pinch these days if they're all shacked up in that dump. Those houses are due for demolition. Most of 'em are already empty. Maybe they're just squatting. Living rent free until they get kicked out.'

'Could be.'

But that was really of no interest to the

chief inspector. All he was interested in was getting the three villains under lock and key. And maybe — just maybe — finding where a stack of gold bars was hidden.

'The stuff has to be somewhere. It can't just have evaporated. My guess is it's still where Brogan hid it. And the question is — did he reveal the secret before he was snuffed out or didn't he?'

It was the sixty thousand dollar question. Or even a lot more than that. The devil of a lot more. And they had no answer.

★ ★ ★

The murder on its premises, far from putting customers off, had in fact brought an increase of business to the Top Notch, and if you wished for a table it was necessary to book well ahead. The one at which the actual killing had taken place was in particular demand. Such were the ghoulish tastes of certain members of the general public.

For his part, Caley avoided the place; he was determined never to go near it again. He had never been so shocked in his life as he had been when the podgy man had hauled out the pistol and shot Brogan in the head. Well, it was not quite the sort of thing you expected when returning from a visit to the toilet, was it? The sight of poor old Chuck with his nose in the coffee cup and his blood and brains on the cloth was really most unpleasant.

He had never paid for the meal, and he suspected that a number of other customers had left in a hurry without settling their bills either. There had been such chaos, and the waiters must have been as shocked as anyone else. It was hardly something you could describe as being all in the day's work.

He still could not figure out the meaning of that slip of paper which Brogan had entrusted to him for safe keeping. But it had to have been important in Brogan's estimation at least. And what could have been more important to the late but unlamented Chuck than a few bars of shining yellow metal that he had presumably hidden away somewhere? Ergo, it had to do with that. But in what way? Further examination of it and a racking of the brains had brought him no nearer a solution of the conundrum. And meanwhile his financial affairs had taken no turn for the better. Before long, if nothing turned up, he might really be in Queer Street. Mr Micawber had been in daily expectation of something turning up; but he was no Mr M, and he could not console himself with any such self-deluding thought. His one faint hope had stemmed from Brogan's hint of something to his advantage; but the man had snuffed it before he could explain what he had meant by this.

Which was hardly his fault, of course.

But inconvenient, nevertheless.

It had to do with the gold, undoubtedly. What else? And it also had to do with the scrap of paper now residing in the old iron safe in a corner of his office. So maybe he had better take another look at it and do some more racking of the brains.

He did so, and nothing came of it.

So he put the thing back in the safe and lit another cigarette.

★ ★ ★

Meanwhile the investigation into Brogan's murder was proceeding and getting nowhere.

'It was one of those three,' Cartwright said. And he did not need to tell Brown which three he was referring to. 'We know damn well it was. It had to be.'

But they had no proof. And without proof what could you do?

'We'll keep an eye on them,' he said. 'We'll watch them like hawks.'

'And Caley?'

'Him too,' Cartwright said. 'Him bloody too.'

★   ★   ★

The police had paid a visit to Caley's place. Detective Sergeant Brown went along with a detective constable named Sims, a cherub-faced young man with ambitions to rise in the Force. They did not have a search warrant, but Brown asked if there would be any objection to their taking a look around.

Caley needed no telling that it would have been unwise to object. It would seem as though he had something to hide.

So he let them in.

It seemed to him that the look round became a pretty thorough search. He had no idea what they were looking for; and maybe they were no wiser on that point than he was. They found nothing incriminating for the simple reason that there was nothing of that description in the place.

They noticed the safe of course.

'What do you keep in there?' Brown asked.

'Nothing,' Caley said. 'As you can see, it's pretty much scrap iron. The door's locked and I've lost the key.'

'Ah!' Brown said.

Enigmatically.

'So it's in the safe,' Cartwright said.

'What is?' Brown said.

'Whatever it is he's got to hide.'

'If anything.'

'There must be something. People don't lose keys to safes, however old they are.'

'You think we should go back with a search warrant and a locksmith, sir?'

'Waste of time. He'll have shifted it as soon as you left.'

Whatever it was.

If anything.

9

Export-Import

Several months before the shooting at the Top Notch whereby the unfortunate Chuck Brogan lost his worthless life, a married couple named Mr and Mrs Danby were having breakfast together, but not speaking much.

Oliver Danby was thirty-six years old and as handsome as a film star. He had the figure of an athlete and he attracted women like wasps to a honeypot. Perhaps it was the air of maturity that helped; there was nothing gauche about him. And he had money. That helped too.

He had black hair, and it was not receding at the temples or turning grey at the sides. Some people might have thought he really had too much going for him, including a wife who was as attractive in her way as he was in his. Such an idea could of course have been formed by envy. And there were certainly those who did envy him.

There was one thing that perhaps marred the picture of a perfect little family: there were no children. But possibly they had no desire to raise a family; feeling themselves quite content to remain as they were, just the two of them. Children could after all be quite a burden, and maybe this was one they had no wish to shoulder.

The house they occupied was on the outskirts of a small Norfolk village, some thirty miles to the south-east of Norwich. It was a comparatively new house, being only a few years old, one of a group of three which were the kind that estate agents were inclined to describe as executive dwellings. There were five bedrooms, a couple of bathrooms, a kitchen that had everything and a spacious sitting-room. The houses were well separated from one another and each was of a different design from the other two. There were fairly large gardens enclosed by wooden fencing.

Each house had a two-car garage, and the Danbys' was sometimes occupied by their two cars. Danby's was a Range Rover, an off-the-road vehicle which seldom went off the road and guzzled petrol. His wife, Cynthia, drove a Mercedes convertible.

None of the neighbours knew precisely what Danby did for a living, though judging by appearances it had to be something fairly profitable. He never spoke about it; but it was known that he had an office in Norwich and there was a rumour that he was in the export and import line, though what he exported or imported remained a mystery.

It was an odd thing, frequently remarked upon, that the Danbys were scarcely ever seen out together. It was as if, when away from their home, they led quite separate existences. Still, if that was the way they chose to live their lives, it was nobody's business but their own. People talked about them nevertheless; you could not prevent people from talking; especially the neighbours on each side, with whom they were barely on nodding terms.

So, although it was generally agreed that they were a most attractive couple in the physical sense, there was nevertheless something distinctly odd about them.

A snatch of conversation over the breakfast table one morning might have provided some clue to their habits. Or, on the other hand, it might not.

Danby swallowed a mouthful of coffee, set the cup down and said. 'I shall be leaving next Tuesday.'

His wife showed no surprise at this statement. She might well have been expecting it.

'And you will be back when?'

'Expect me when you see me.'

'As usual.'

She asked no further questions. She appeared to be only marginally interested in Danby's proposed leaving and returning. She did not ask where he was going or why. Possibly she already knew.

She undoubtedly knew that he owned a small seagoing yacht which resided when not in use in a marina at what had once been a busy fishing village on the East Anglian coast; a place named Lingburgh. The marina was of no great size and could accommodate only a small number of boats; but Danby had one of the berths reserved for his exclusive use, even though he might frequently vacate it for indefinite periods of time.

Cynthia never went near the place and had never set foot on the deck of *Osprey*, which was the name of the yacht. She hated sailing. In her youth she had once been taken for a sea trip in a small boat, had been vilely sick and had vowed never in any circumstances to repeat the experience. Which made it all the more odd that she should have married a man who was such a dedicated sailor. Perhaps it had been because Danby had fallen madly in love with her on sight and had swept her off her feet. Perhaps she had been eager to become independent of her family and had been dazzled by the apparent wealth of the suitor. For whatever reason, they had undoubtedly married in haste, and if they had not exactly repented at leisure, had soon found that first fine careless rapture becoming a trifle ragged around the edges.

Yet they had stayed together, possibly because it suited them both to do so and neither could be bothered to force a break which would have seemed quite unnecessary when each could go his or her own way regardless of the other.

'You will be going to the office today?'

'Yes.'

She lit a cigarette. She was wearing a silk kimono and no make-up. Even so, at this time in the morning she looked great. To himself Danby had to admit as much. So why had they drifted so far apart? He could think of no logical explanation. It was just one of those things. It happened and you had to accept it.

'I wonder you bother,' she said.

'Oh,' he said, 'it's no bother, I assure you.'

She detected a note of mockery in his voice, but she did not remark on it. They knew each other so well these days; could almost read the other one's thoughts. Which was perhaps no great advantage to the relationship.

* * *

He drove to Norwich in the Range Rover, avoiding the main road. He found it more pleasant to stick to the meandering minor roads that were little more than country lanes for parts of the way, twisting and turning from village to village. He was not in any hurry and took no delight in speed for speed's sake. There had been a time in his younger days when he would have driven like Jehu, ignoring speed limits and getting a kick from it. But that was all in the past, and the risks he took now were of quite a different character; more serious certainly, but necessary. Eliminate the hazards and you could wave goodbye to the expensive life style. It was a choice he had made and it was his intention to stick to it; for the present at least.

He had as usual timed his journey late enough to avoid the morning rush when from the outskirts of the city you moved forward at a snail's pace and breathed the exhaust fumes from other vehicles. Instead, he coasted in and made his way without serious hindrance to the tall modern building in which he had his office.

He left the Range Rover in the basement car park and rode up in the lift to the third floor, walked some twenty yards down a corridor and came to the door of his own office. A plate on one side indicated in tasteful gold lettering that this was the head-quarters of O.P. Danby Limited, Export-Import.

Anyone else entering the office as he now did might have been surprised to discover how little business appeared to be taking place inside. It was not large. Indeed, for an export and import enterprise of any importance it might have been considered very small. It was, however, adequately equipped for the use of anyone desiring to carry on something of the kind in a modest sort of way. There was a handsome desk on which were two tele-phones, a computer, an in-tray and an out-tray, each holding a few token sheets of paper, a few ball-point pens, a scribbling pad and a perpetual calendar. An up-to-date Whitaker's Almanack and a Guide to London were in such pristine condition that it seemed doubt-ful whether they had ever been used.

Seated behind this desk on a well-padded swivel-chair was the sole occupant of the office: a young woman who could not have been much more than twenty years old. To supplement her youthfulness there were more physical attributes such as long blonde hair, a delightful face, sapphire blue eyes, Cupid's bow lips and a slightly retroussé nose. Her figure when she jumped up from the chair, as she did when Danby came in, could be seen to be as near perfection as anyone might wish. She was wearing a cream-coloured woollen jumper and a black miniskirt, which revealed the greater part of a pair of legs that any woman might have been proud to reveal.

Her greeting of Danby as he came in was hardly the normal kind for a secretary on the entry of the boss; which role was presumably his. She ran to him, flung her arms round his neck and gave him a smacking kiss on the lips. The fact that he showed no surprise at this seemed to indicate that it was not in any way unusual. Indeed, he returned hug for hug.

'You're late,' she said when finally he released her. 'Did you get held up?'

'No. I started late. What have you been doing?'

'Reading. What else do you think?'

There was a romantic novel lying on the desk where she had dropped it when Danby came in. She was an avid reader of romances and spent much of her time in the office doing just that when she was not watching television on a set that was part of the office furniture.

'So what shall we do today?' Danby said.

She gave a shrug. 'I don't know. You suggest something.'

'Well, it's a nice day. I thought we might go to the races. Have a bit of a flutter on the gee-gees. What do you say?'

'Sounds great. Where are the races?'

'Newmarket. Where else? Okay?'

'Okay.'

'Let's go then.'

10

Don't Fix It

She was the sole employee of O.P. Danby Limited, Export-Import. Her name was Angela Crowe and she lived in a small bed-sitter which had been described by the advertiser as a studio flat. Her duties with the firm were scarcely onerous. Each day, except weekends, she would arrive at the office at nine o'clock, open up and spend the rest of the day, if Danby failed to put in an appearance, reading one of the many romances with which she provided herself or watching chat shows and soaps on television. Between one o'clock and two she would go for lunch at a restaurant in the city, and at five p.m. she would lock up and go home.

When Danby was away for any length of time she would, in the unlikely event of anyone ringing up to make an enquiry, inform the caller that he was abroad on business at present and she could not tell precisely when he would be back. This would in fact be the truth, since she had no idea of what Danby did when he was overseas. All she knew was that he went alone and went in his yacht *Osprey*. He had never volunteered any information beyond that, and she had never asked for any. It was, she reflected, none of her business, and if he had wished to tell her about it he would have done so. But he had not, so that was that.

One thing was certain: she was well rewarded for what she did, and she could think of no other job she could have obtained with her somewhat limited qualifications that would have been nearly as rewarding as the one she had. She knew she was in luck when Danby picked her out of a number of hopeful young ladies who had applied for the position that had been advertised. She soon realised that it was not her ability regarding secretarial matters that had ensured her success in competition with the others, and she could only conclude that it had been her personality; or, to put it another way, her sexual appeal to the male animal. Moreover, she had not long been at what could hardly be called work before realising that the office was no more than a front which her employer, for some reason that was still a mystery to her, felt obliged to present to the world at large. Why he should have wished to do so she could not for the life of her figure out. So perhaps it was just a whim of his; a piece of harmless eccentricity which amused him and gave offence to no one.

People, she reflected, were not all made alike. And she thanked her lucky stars that they were not.

★   ★   ★

It could not have been a more pleasant day for going to the Newmarket races. The sun shone, the air was balmy and there was not a hint of rain forecast. Such days came all too rarely in the British climate and, as Danby remarked, it was only sensible to take advantage of them when they did.

They went in the Range Rover, and Danby let Angela drive for part of the way. She had a driving licence but no car of her own. She had once owned a rather ancient Mini, but had had an accident from which the car had emerged as a complete wreck. No one else had been involved; she had skidded on an icy road and the car had tried to wrap itself round a tree. Fortunately her own injuries had been slight: a sprained ankle and a few bruises, but she had not yet saved up enough money to buy another car. Nevertheless, she loved driving, and the Range Rover was quite a step up from the Mini.

Traffic on the A11 was hellish as usual, and

just before they reached Barton Mills Danby took over the wheel. Soon they were at the Heath and there were horses to be seen here and there.

'I love to see them,' Angela said. 'They're so pretty, don't you think?'

It was not the word Danby would have used to describe them, but he let it pass.

★   ★   ★

They arrived in Newmarket in time for lunch. The town was crowded and there were lots of horsey-looking people milling around, including a sprinkling of little men with bandy legs who might have been stable lads or superannuated jockeys. There was even a horse here and there, being led by its halter.

'Do they do anything here that isn't connected with racing?' Angela asked.

Danby gave a laugh. 'You might not imagine so, but I suppose there are other activities, though I don't know what. Mention Newmarket and all you think of is horses.'

They took their time over lunch and were too late at the course for the first race of the meeting. The second race was about to start when they found a place by the rails.

'There's a thing about racing,' Angela said. 'More than half the time is spent waiting around for the next race. Then the horses go past in a flash and that's it. I wonder what it is that grabs people. Is it just the betting?'

'No,' Danby said. 'There's more to it than that. You can bet off course, in a betting shop, but it's not the same. There's a kind of magic in a race meeting.'

'But it's not everybody's cup of tea, is it?'

'True. It's mostly lower and upper class who go for it. The middle class tend to stay away. Maybe they disapprove of gambling. A Puritan hangover.'

'But you're middle class, aren't you?'

He gave a laugh. 'Touché! I was making a sweeping statement, and they're generally wrong. But anyway, people who've got work to do can't spend their time on a racecourse.'

'Unless they're jockeys.'

'Or trainers.'

'Or bookies.'

'Or tipsters.'

Angela herself had been accosted by a tipster; a skinny, weather-beaten character with a face like an apple that had been too long on the shelf. He offered her an envelope in which he assured her was the winner of the three-thirty. He said it was a gift at one nicker; and she fell for his spiel because, as she told Danby later, she felt sorry for him.

'He looked so undernourished.'

84

'You've been conned,' Danby said. 'It'll be a rank outsider.'

It was; but it came home at fifty to one, and Angela crowed.

'This is my lucky day. And you don't know everything.'

It was Danby's practice to give her twenty-five pounds whenever they went to a race meeting. It was for her to use as betting money. She usually lost it all. But this was an exception. She was two hundred and sixty pounds to the good at the end of the day and could hardly contain her delight.

'I wonder,' she said, 'whether that poor man who tipped me the horse backed it himself.'

'Of course not. Tipsters don't back no-hopers.'

'But it wasn't a no-hoper, was it?'

'As things turned out, no. Maybe the other horses were nobbled.'

She gave his arm a squeeze. 'Now you're being nasty. Just because you backed losers.'

She was not altogether wrong at that. Danby was a man who hated losing. In everything he did he had to be a winner; that was his creed; it had been so from childhood onward. And if coming out top sometimes entailed ways and means that were more than a little questionable, well, so be it. That was the way of the world, and devil take the hindmost.

* * *

They had a meal on the way home at The Bell in Thetford, an old coaching hostelry that had been in the business for centuries, and then drove back to the office in Norwich. It was getting pretty late by then and business in the building had virtually finished for the day.

Nevertheless, they went up to the third floor office which ostensibly served as headquarters of the export-import firm of O.P. Danby Limited, let themselves in and locked the door behind them.

There was, besides the main section where Miss Crowe spent a good deal of her time doing very little that could be accurately described as work, another, much smaller room on the right, with a door panelled with frosted glass. The chief piece of furniture in this room was a sofa large enough to serve as a bed if so required. On the left of this, screened by more frosted glass, was a washroom with a water closet and a shower.

Danby and Miss Crowe did not linger in the main office but went straight to the smaller room, as if by mutual consent. There was a drinks cabinet in this room, and for a time they sat on the sofa, Danby with a glass of whisky and water in his hand and Angela with one of gin and tonic.

The drinks finished, again as if following a well-established practice, they stripped to the buff and made energetic love on the sofa. Had there been anyone in the outer office, the sound of Miss Crowe's cries of ecstasy would surely have been audible to them. But there was no one, and they were able to enjoy their embraces with no fear of interruption or restraint.

Later they shared the curtained enclosure of the shower and emerged refreshed.

'We should do this more often,' Danby said.

'That would be nice.'

'Nice certainly, but in the circumstances not really practical, I'm afraid.'

And then he told her what he had already told Cynthia. 'I shall be going away next Tuesday.'

Her reaction was different from the other woman's. She looked disappointed. 'Do you really have to?'

'Yes, I do. It can't be helped.'

'I shall miss you.'

It was the truth. He was perhaps fifteen or more years older than this girl, but she was in love with him. Sometimes she wondered whether he was really in love with her, and she could not be sure. It might simply be that she gave him what he wanted — youth and beauty and a gorgeous body. And for the present maybe that was enough.

'I should be sorry if you didn't,' he said.

'When will you be back?'

'That,' he said, 'is in the lap of the gods. Who can tell? Hold the fort while I'm away.'

Sometimes, even often in fact, the question would return to her mind regarding where he went on his trips abroad and how he got the money to rent an office where no business was transacted and employ a secretary who did little but read romantic novels and watch television. But still she did not ask questions on these points because she knew she would get no satisfactory answer and might only succeed in annoying the man.

★ ★ ★

He took her back to her studio flat after they left the office and then returned to the house he shared with his lawfully wedded wife, Cynthia.

He noticed that there was no Mercedes in the garage and that the house was in darkness. But it did not bother him. It was getting on for midnight and Cynthia was obviously still out somewhere. He had a shrewd idea of where she was and with whom; but she could do as she pleased and he had no intention of interfering. This was the pattern of their lives and it worked well enough, so why make trouble? If it ain't broke don't fix it, as the saying was.

He let himself into the empty house, made himself a nightcap, drank it and went to bed.

11

Progress

It was a measure of the quality of Alan Caley's mental processes that it took him almost a week before he realised that the slip of paper which Brogan had given him in the envelope was a rough sketch map of some part of the country. Admittedly it was a pretty crude piece of work, but nevertheless he now had no doubt that this was what it was.

And then, with rather less delay, he came to the conclusion that it had to be a clue to the whereabouts of the place where Brogan had hidden the gold bullion, in all likelihood underground.

But why had he drawn it? The only possible answer to this question that he could think of was that Brogan had feared his memory might not be fully reliable after a lengthy stay in prison. Possibly he thought that incarceration might have a deleterious effect on the brain; as a result of which he himself might forget the exact location of the place where he had hidden the loot.

That seemed logical, and Caley felt he could run with it.

But then the next question that arose was this: why had he given it to Caley to keep?

Because he feared he might not be able to hold on to it safely himself?

Perhaps. But why?

Because he was afraid the gang, Tulley, Harker and Starke, might take it from him? Almost certainly.

Which could only mean that he had had no intention of sharing the loot with his former partners in crime. And after having done his time in prison while they remained free as air, that appeared to be a perfectly understandable way of looking at things.

Yet this still failed to explain why he had given the map to Caley to keep. Unless he was afraid, with pretty good reason when you came to think about it, that they might manhandle him, search him and find the map on his person.

Well, he could have hidden it somewhere, could he not?

Yes, to be sure he could. But there was surely more to it than that. He would not have dared to go for the gold himself because he knew that not only the police but those three gangsters would be watching his every move and waiting to pounce on him as soon as he started digging. So he had to get somebody else to fetch the stuff for him, and the only somebody he could think of was his erstwhile semi-buddie. Alan Caley, as ever was.

So why on earth had he been so secretive? Why had he not told Caley what was in the envelope and what his plan was?

Well, maybe having gone so far he still could not yet bring himself to reveal all. In Caley's pocket he felt that the map was safe, and it would buy him time to make up his mind whether or not to trust the only person he could think of who might agree to his proposal and not go running to the coppers to spill the beans. Yet even of Caley, almost on his beam-ends and in dire need of an injection of folding money, he still could not be absolutely certain.

So he had hesitated, and the hesitation had proved terminal.

★ ★ ★

When he had worked all this out Caley felt quite pleased with himself. So he was not such a dunce after all. He might be a bit slow but he got there in the end. One had to remember that it was the tortoise that won the race with the hare.

And then another thought came into his head; and this almost made him giddy with exultation. For the thought was the realisation that he might now have in his possession the clue, the pointer, the signpost to a fortune in gold bullion. And it would all be his, every last cent of it. He wondered what the value of it was. He had no idea; but it had to be a great deal, a very great deal; enough to keep him in the lap of luxury for the rest of his life. A man could be excused for feeling quite delirious with such a prospect revealing itself before his dazzled eyes.

* * *

The delirium lasted less than five minutes. That was how long it took him to light a cigarette, take half a dozen puffs of the weed and examine once again Brogan's wretched map.

Then his heart sank; for how on earth was he to interpret it? The thing was not only crude; it was so damned cryptic. To the man himself it had probably seemed as clear as daylight; but he had drawn it and presumably knew what the symbols represented. To Caley few of them conveyed any information. The spidery lines were no doubt roads; of that he could be reasonably certain. At certain places along these lines were clusters of tiny rectangles which puzzled him for quite a time before it occurred to him that they probably represented villages or small towns. Moreover, beside each group was a capital letter. There were four of these: D G H and O; which were possibly, or even probably, the initial letters of the names of the towns or villages.

Having come to this conclusion, he felt that he was making progress. He lit another cigarette and remembered that in the newspaper report of Brogan's murder there had been a brief account of the original bullion theft. He had kept the cutting and referred to it now. It refreshed his memory that the theft had taken place in East Anglia. For some reason or other, not divulged, the gold ingots had been temporarily stored in a strong room in one of the buildings on a former RAF station. Apparently they were to be shipped later to the Continent from one of the east coast ports. The thieves had taken only a part of the bullion; maybe because this was as much as they could carry away or because they feared they might be apprehended if they did not leave quickly.

'Ah!' Caley muttered.

He recalled that Brogan, whose job had obviously been to transport the haul to

94

wherever they intended it should be hidden until they could dispose of it had been driving a white Ford van, and they would not have wanted to overload it. Not having too large an amount would have made Brogan's task of burying the stuff less difficult; but the value of it could still have been high. Journalistic estimates varied widely. Some put it as high as a hundred million. Caley doubted whether such a figure was a likely one; but that there was a fortune waiting for him if only he could locate it he had no doubt.

The newspaper report recalled that there had been a watchman at the place where the gold had been stored, and it was suspected that he had been in league with the gang. If this were so it was certain that they had treated him very badly. It had been all very well to tie and gag him and inflict superficial injuries, but they had gone much further. They had broken an arm and a rib and had beaten the unfortunate man so severely about the head that he had been knocked unconscious and had lost all memory of the events on the night in question. Caley made a guess that the one who had done most of the damage had been Harker. It was he who had shot Brogan, and it was obvious that he had an unpredictable temper and was apt to lose control of himself. Which was not the most pleasant of thoughts to enter the head of one who was even now preparing to cheat the gang of three.

But it did not deter him. The prize that might possibly be his far outweighed all other considerations.

'I must get it,' he told himself. 'I must. I have to.'

Without it the vision of his future appeared bleak indeed.

It seemed that the alarm system had been switched off and the strong room inside the building had been broken open with an oxyacetylene cutter which had been abandoned at the scene when the gang made their getaway. No fingerprints had been left on anything, so it was assumed that the men had all worn gloves, possibly the rubber variety. Which had been very frustrating for the police; of whom one had been the then Detective Sergeant Stephen Cartwright.

★   ★   ★

Caley stared again at Brogan's sketch map. He noticed that, situated a little way outside the triangle of lines that had to be roads, were three marks that looked rather like arrows, each with a straight stem capped by a kind of inverted V. He was puzzled by these for a time; but then it came to him that perhaps they represented a small group of trees. Close to them were the letters SB, which he guessed might refer to the kind of tree they represented. He was not very well versed on the subject of timber except when it came in the shape of sawn planks, and he could not even make a guess at what SB might stand for. But he noticed next that close to these markings was a very small cross; so small indeed that he had overlooked it at first. But now it came to his attention and again he uttered that brief exclamation.

'Ah!'

For a while he was almost beside himself with delight, and he even danced a little jig in celebration. For might it not be that this tiny cross, hardly big enough to see without a magnifying glass, marked the spot where Brogan had buried the gold? Surely it had to be.

But once again there followed the reaction, and he sank back into black depression. For what, after all, had he discovered? Nothing but a tiny cross on a scrap of paper which might or might not mark the spot where a treasure lay buried.

For he had not the faintest idea where that spot was in actual fact. True, he had a map of sorts; that could not be denied. But what a map! It was useless to him as long as he remained ignorant of the whereabouts of that portion of land to which it referred. He could not even tell how large or how small that portion was, since Brogan had not been obliging enough to append a scale. Those meandering roads might be several miles long or they might be merely a few hundred yards. It was all so frustrating.

Caley sighed. He failed to see how he could progress further. Perhaps the best course would be to put the damned thing away for the present and have another go at it next day.

12

Triangles

The next day he had an idea. He went to the nearest public library and consulted a book on trees. It took very little time then to conclude that the SB had to stand for silver birch. It seemed so obvious now, and the bonus was that the silver birch was just about the only tree he could recognise with any degree of certainty.

Now, he thought, I am really making progress. It was amazing what a good night's sleep could do for the brain.

It had in fact been a sleep full of dreams of digging up treasure, of holding bars of gold in his hands. Which might have been fine if Slim Harker, Josh Tulley and Lugs Starke, the last with ears of truly monstrous size, had not kept appearing. Chuck Brogan too, all alive and well again, apart from a gaping hole in the head which everyone else appeared to regard as entirely natural.

Once again, however, the feeling of euphoria did not last long. Another examination of Brogan's map revealed the depressing fact that, though he might have identified three silver birch trees as being markers of the resting place of the gold, he still had not the faintest idea of where the trees were situated. It was not as if silver birches were a rarity; you came across them everywhere; and it was hardly practical to go around digging great holes wherever three of the kind happened to be grouped together.

'Damn you, Chuck,' he muttered. 'Why the devil couldn't you have given me a clue?'

But of course Brogan had never intended the map to be deciphered by anyone else; it had been designed simply as an aide-mémoire for himself. He had fully expected to be all alive and kicking in order to give Caley verbal directions regarding the whereabouts of the treasure when the time came. And the time never had come; nor would it ever come now. So Caley would have to work out all the answers for himself. He could never enlist the help of anyone smarter than he was without giving the game away. It was truly depressing to feel himself so near and yet so far from a fortune of which he was in such dire need.

Yet again he sought consolation and perhaps inspiration in a cigarette.

And after a few more lungsful of the cancer-breeding smoke he did in fact have an idea. All he needed to do would be to examine a map of East Anglia to discover where there were roads forming a rough triangle and see which of these appeared to match Brogan's sketch.

He had no such map in the house, so he would have to buy one. To do that he would need to visit a bookshop; something he had not done for years, since his reading was pretty well limited to the tabloid press and some of the junk mail that came tumbling through his letterbox every day.

*　*　*

He took the pick-up truck, and it was not long before he noticed a police car on his tail. It gave his heart a jolt. He could never see a police car these days without a feeling of guilt. Which was ridiculous, because he had done nothing illegal — yet. Apart, of course, from withholding certain information that might have helped them with their enquiries. Like the fact that he possessed a possible key to the whereabouts of a load of gold bullion, which he proposed to use to his own advantage if he could only solve the puzzle he was working on.

The car on his tail proved that they were still keeping an eye on him; and he did not like it. He had seen nothing during these last few days of Harker and Tulley and Starke, but he did not try to kid himself that they had forgotten him. Like the coppers, they would have it in their heads that Brogan had told him a lot more than he was admitting. They were lying low for the present, but one of these days he would have a visit from them; of that he felt sure. And they might be worse than the police; because they were villains and would feel no obligation to stick to the letter of the law when it came to interrogating him. They might resort to physical means to extract information. And these means might well be painful.

It bothered him of course. He would have needed to be far more courageous than he was if it had not. And if the prize had not been so indispensable to him he might have been inclined to give them the sketch map and let them work it out for themselves if they were smart enough. Which he doubted.

But that sweet vision of riches beyond his wildest dreams which had loomed up before his eyes served to put new strength into his backbone and made him willing to face even the prospect of a going-over by such vile characters as those with some degree of fortitude.

There was of course another problem lying in wait for him. Even if he did eventually discover the gold and carry it back to his place, how did he dispose of it? One could hardly drive up to a bank with a truckload of gold ingots and offer to exchange them for a million or two pounds sterling in currency notes. You could not even invest the stuff in shares on the stock market without awkward questions being asked. Presumably the gang had had some plan for marketing it; but they were criminals and would certainly have ways and means that were not available to him.

He recognised that this was a difficulty that would present itself after he had found and helped himself to the cache of precious metal; but he brushed it aside. When the time came he would surely think of some way round the problem. The idea of sharing the loot with the three who had originally stolen it entered his head and was immediately dismissed. Even if they made a bargain by which they undertook to market the gold and pay him a quarter or so of the proceeds, would they honour the agreement? Not on your life! They would grab the lot and he could sing for his supper.

But suppose he brought pressure on them by threatening to blow the gaff, run to the coppers and tell them all? Well, that was another horse that would never run. And why? Because they had the means of silencing him; the way Chuck Brogan had been silenced with a hole in the head. That was why.

* * *

He noticed that the police car was no longer on his tail; it had turned away down a side street. So maybe it had not been following him after all. Maybe he was getting too jumpy. The coppers might be keeping an eye on him, but they could hardly follow him around wherever he went. They had other duties to perform, and there was no sense in getting paranoid about it.

'They'll have eased up by now,' he reflected. 'They can't spend all their time sitting on my tail. They've got better things to do.'

But it still gave him a mild shock whenever he caught sight of a blue uniform. It was what a guilty conscience did for you.

* * *

He found a bookshop and bought a road map of the Eastern Counties and took it home to that old house which had once been bright and welcoming but had now become no more than a depressing refuge for its last remaining occupant.

He opened the map at once, spreading it out on the desk in his office. It was large scale and all the roads were there; every last one of them.

And he was appalled.

It seemed as if all the minor roads and lanes in the whole of East Anglia formed themselves into rough triangles in some parts of their meanderings. These formations were spread out across the entire area, and they were of all sizes from very small to very large. The one thing they had in common was that they were three-sided and that none of them appeared to bear much resemblance to the map that Brogan had drawn.

Caley's heart sank as he stared at the map with its seemingly endless supply of triangles. It was hopeless. It was just bloody well hopeless. He could have wept with frustration.

13

Martine

Detective Chief Inspector Stephen Cartwright was a much disgruntled man. The investigation into the murder of Chuck Brogan appeared to have run into the sands and little progress was being made. The Top Notch, so he had heard, was doing good business, but that did not help him.

What really needled him was the fact that he was quite certain the killer was one of three men: Lugs Starke, Slim Harker or Josh Tulley. Yet he could not pin it on any one of them. He felt convinced too that this Alan Caley character was holding out on him. He would have made a bet that the man knew a lot more than he would admit; like the identity of the two men who had visited Brogan's table while he had been in the toilet. Very convenient, that visit to the toilet. It might almost have been prearranged.

He mentioned the theory to Detective Sergeant Brown, but found no support there. Brown thought it was going a little too far; though he did not say so. He felt that the chief inspector was letting himself become rather too obsessed with this case and his desire to nail the three men.

'We'll get them all in the end,' he said. 'If not for this, then for something else.'

'It won't be the same,' Cartwright said. 'It just won't be the same.'

And of course it would not if it was just plain burglary or robbery with violence or grievous bodily harm. None of these had quite the feel of murder, though the latter two could be very nasty when it came to the point.

Anyway, there were other matters to attend to. You could not keep everyone engaged on a murder investigation that had gone cold. And you could not take men from other duties just to keep an eye on people like Caley and the three gangsters. A balance had to be struck, whether Cartwright liked it or not.

★ ★ ★

So, if Caley had only known it, he might have been more easy in his mind regarding police surveillance. For though Cartwright would continue to keep him in mind, as well as the other three, they would no longer be watched as closely as heretofore.

It was, for instance, never reported that

Caley had gone into a branch of W.H. Smith and purchased a road map of the Eastern Counties, which he had carried home with him.

If Cartwright had known this it might have given him food for thought. But he had not known it, and the thought went under-nourished.

★ ★ ★

Later that day Caley had a visitor. It was his ever-loving, or maybe now not so loving, wife, Martine.

It was an unexpected visit. He had scarcely had a glimpse of her since the breaking up of their marriage. And he had not missed her; any more, that is, than he would have missed a piece of furniture that had been removed. She did not knock; she just opened the back door, which had not been locked, and walked in. He heard the sound and came to see who could have made it.

'You!' he said.

'Yes,' she said. 'Me. You don't sound overjoyed to see me.'

'Should I be?'

'Well, absence is supposed to make the heart grow fonder, isn't it?'

'You didn't come here to tell me that.'

'No, of course I didn't. What if I told you I came to see how you were getting along all on your ownsome?'

He doubted whether this was the true reason for her visit, but he let it go.

'I'm managing.'

'Well, you would, wouldn't you?' And then: 'You've really got yourself into the public eye now, haven't you. Well and truly in.'

'How do you mean?' Caley asked. But of course he knew.

'Why, you've been in the news, haven't you? And not really for the best of reasons.'

'Ah!'

'Look,' she said, 'there's no point in standing here like a couple of prats. Why don't we go into the lounge? And maybe you could offer me a cup of tea. You've still got some, I suppose?'

He hesitated, but only momentarily. He could hardly refuse, though he had no desire for a lengthy tête-á-tête.

'Very well. You go ahead and I'll make the tea.'

When he had made it he poured out two cups and found some chocolate biscuits which were not as crisp as they had once been. He carried all these on a tray into the room which she called the lounge but had always been known in his parents' time as the front room. She was sitting in an armchair which was one of a three-piece suite — two chairs and a sofa — beginning to look a trifle worn after a good many years of use.

He carried the tray to her and she took one of the cups and a biscuit which she nibbled.

'Quite the housekeeper now, aren't you, Alan?'

He shrugged. 'I have to be, don't I?'

He set the tray down on a side-table, took a cup of tea for himself and sat in the second armchair, facing her. She was, he thought, putting on weight and probably hating it. He had never noticed it before. She was not as pretty as she had been when he had fallen for her charms; but that was only to be expected. Her features had coarsened and there was the hint of a double chin.

She was wearing a pink jumper and white slacks, with high-heeled shoes, open-toed. The slacks were a mistake; they accentuated the size of her bottom, which had never been one of her more attractive features.

'So you read all about it,' Caley said.

'I could hardly avoid it, could I?'

'Well anyway, you took your time in coming to see me. It didn't happen yesterday, did it?'

'I thought I'd give things time to settle down.'

He made no comment on that.

'People are talking, you know,' she said. And sniffed.

'People always talk. Let them.'

'Well, it's not very nice for me, is it?'

'I can't see what in hell it matters to you.'

She gave a toss of the head. 'Now isn't that just typical of you. Thinking only of yourself. And you don't need to swear.'

'Anyway, it's over and done with as far as I'm concerned,' Caley said.

Which of course was very far from the truth. But he had no intention of telling her that.

'What I can't understand,' she said, 'is why you ever went to that restaurant for lunch with a man like this Chuck Brogan. You must have been crazy.'

'I went because he invited me. And we were at school together.'

'And of course that makes it quite all right.' She spoke sarcastically. 'No matter that the old school pal was an ex-con who'd taken part in a plot to steal a fortune in gold bars. A man who gets himself shot in the head while he's waiting for you to come back from the loo.' She made it sound as though this too was a crime perpetrated by the victim.

'I'm sure he didn't plan to be.'

'Oh, really? You surprise me. But I take it

his plan was to give you a free lunch?'

'Yes. He rang me up and invited me.'

'I suppose he couldn't find anyone else who would accept the invitation.'

'I don't know. Does it matter?'

'It matters to me. How do you think I feel when people ask me what my husband has been up to?'

'I haven't the least idea how you feel,' Caley said. 'The fact is I haven't given it a thought.'

'And isn't that just typical too!'

Caley took a packet of cigarettes from his pocket and lit one.

'So,' Martine said, 'you've started smoking again. I'd have thought you could have found a better use for your money.'

'Such as?'

'Such as providing for your wife. Which I still am, you know. And I have to live on something.'

He had expected this. It was probably the reason why she had paid him a visit. But it was no more welcome for having been foreseen. There had been a faint hope in his mind that now she had gone back to her parents they might provide for her; but perhaps they were not terribly keen on the idea and would rather not have had her thrown back on their hands. So maybe

Martine was feeling the pinch.

Well, she was not the only one.

'So you walk out on me and still expect me to meet all your expenses. Is that it?'

She sniffed again. He wondered whether she had a cold or whether it was simply a habit.

'Like I said, I'm still your wife.'

'And where do you think I'm going to find the money?'

'Why don't you sell your story to one of the papers?'

'What story?'

'About your relationship with this man Brogan.'

'I didn't have a relationship with him.'

'You could make something up.'

'They'd never buy it. I haven't even been approached.'

'You could approach them.'

'It would be pointless. And anyway, even if there was a story I wouldn't want to sell it. I've had enough publicity already.'

'Now isn't that just like you again. There's no go in you.'

She nibbled some more of the biscuit, spilling crumbs, while Caley drew on his cigarette and watched her in silence.

'Anyway,' she said, 'I need some money. Are you going to give me any?'

'Where do you think I'm going to get it?

I'm as pushed as you are. Maybe more so.'

'Is that the truth?'

'Of course it is. Why would I tell a lie?'

'So why don't you sell this place? It would fetch quite a bit, I should think.'

'And then where would I live?'

It was in fact a last resort that he had felt threatening him; the end of something he had known from childhood. But he did not tell her that.

'You could rent a bed-sit or go into lodgings, couldn't you?'

'And live on what? My capital? That wouldn't last long.'

'Well of course you'd need to get a job.'

'Why don't you get one?'

She had no answer to that. She drank some tea to wash the biscuit down and just sat watching him.

In the end, to get rid of her, he managed to scrape up twenty pounds and give it to her. Grudgingly.

It did not satisfy her, of course. How far, she demanded, would a measly twenty pounds go?

'You'll have to think of something, Alan. You really will.'

He was thinking of something; thinking very hard. But of course he could not tell her about that. It was a secret he had to keep very strictly to himself.

14

Bingo!

Caley was looking out of his office window when the car drove into the yard. He knew he was in trouble when the three men got out of it. The car was an old Renault, the only one they had now that their finances were in such a poor state of health.

Previously, apart from that brief glimpse of Tulley and Harker when the shooting took place at the Top Notch, he had observed these men only through the one-way glass when they had been hauled in for the identity parade. Now they had come to see him, and it did not make him happy. It was a visit he had been expecting — and dreading.

He stepped back from the window, but he guessed that it was already too late; they would have spotted him. A moment later they had all walked up to the back door and one of them was hammering away with the old iron knocker.

He regretted now that he had given up locking the gate that gave access to the yard from the street. It had always been secured at night when he had been in business and there was building material to be stolen. But now that there was nothing worth taking he had not bothered. So the police and the gang of three had had no trouble in making their entry. Not that this would really have deterred them. They could easily have come to the front door which opened onto the street.

He did not answer the knocking at once, and it was repeated even more violently, aided by a bit of kicking which made the door shake. It was obvious that the visitors were not going to be put off by any refusal on his part to open the door. If necessary they might be prepared to break it down.

So he went to let them in.

'You took your time,' Starke said. 'You deaf or something?'

Without waiting for an invitation they were walking in. They seemed to guess the layout of the house and they went straight through to the sitting-room and sat down. Caley had to follow them, but he remained standing, ill-at-ease.

'What do you want?'

'As if you didn't know,' Tulley said. 'We want to know what Chuck told you before he kicked the bucket.'

'Told me?'

'About the gold. Like where he'd hidden it.'

'He didn't say anything about that.'

Which was the truth.

'So whose idea was it to have this little get-together at the Top Notch? Yours or his?'

'His.'

'And he never mentioned the gold?'

'No. Why would he?'

'Well, look at it this way. He comes outa stir arter a long spell inside and one of the first things he does is invite an old acquaintance to have lunch with him. Not his one-time buddies. Not us, see? But you. Don't that seem a bit strange.'

'Not really. We were at school together.'

Tulley sneered. 'And what you talked about was the dear old school days. Is that what you're telling me?'

'Mostly.'

'Ah, come off it. Chuck wouldn't have given a damn about the dear old school. So let's have it. What else was there?'

Caley decided to reveal a little more in order to mask the really important part — the confiding of the sketch map to his care. 'Well, he did say that he might tell me something that would perhaps be to my advantage.'

'Ah! Now we're getting somewhere. To your advantage, hey? Moneywise, did he say?'

'No, he didn't. But that's what I took him to mean. He knew I was not doing too well with the business.'

'So how was you to get your pugs on this here money? Did he tell you that?'

'No. He never got round to it. Maybe he would have done if he'd been given the time. But things were cut a bit short, weren't they?'

'Damn right, they were,' Starke said. And once again he shot a venomous glance at Harker, who avoided looking at him.

Starke turned and spoke to Tulley. He sounded impatient.

'This bastard's holding out on us. I bet Chuck told him something, and I bet it was where to look for the gold.'

'No,' Caley said. 'He told me nothing.'

But the denial sounded weak and he could tell they were not accepting it.

Starke got up suddenly. He took two steps and seized Caley's right arm. With surprising strength he twisted it up behind Caley's back, making the joints creak and bringing a cry of pain from the victim.

'I could break it,' Starke said.

Caley believed him.

He was not good at withstanding pain, and he feared that if these thugs resorted to extreme measures he would be forced to cave in and show them the map. But even if he did, would they be any better than he was at deciphering it? They did not look like the kind who would be overburdened with brains; so he doubted it. They might fail to get as near a solution as he had.

Fortunately for him, it did not come to the point, because Tulley intervened.

'Hold it, Lugs. Nobody needs to get his arm broke. I'm sure our Mr Caley will see reason when he's had time to think things over. So what I suggest is we give him a few more days before we really get to work on him.'

He seemed to have some influence with Starke, who with a certain degree of reluctance released Caley and moved away from him; still angry but controlling himself.

'How much longer you reckon we should give him?' Harker said.

Tulley shrugged. 'Oh, let's not fix a date. Let's just say it won't be all that long, and in the meantime he better get his memory going and have something to give us when we call around again. Wotcher say to that, Mr Caley?'

Caley said nothing. He could see that what he was being offered was no more than a reprieve. He was being given time to reflect on what might happen when they came again if he still held back information that they were still convinced he possessed regarding the pot of gold which the three of them had been so long waiting for. Tulley must have been reasoning that a threat hanging over Caley for an unknown period of time might so play on his nerves that when they visited him again he would have come to the conclusion that for his own good he had better not be stubborn.

They went away after that. Caley watched from the window as they piled into the Renault and drove out of the yard, Tulley at the wheel.

He did not like the way things were going. He wondered just how much time they would give him before they came again and resorted to more extreme measures if he still held out on them. His arm ached from the twisting that Starke had given it; and that was only a taste of what might come next time. In his mind he pictured various tortures such men might resort to, and it brought him out in a cold sweat just thinking of them.

So in the end would he have to give in? Even before they got to work on him. After all, would it not be far worse to suffer the torture and finally be forced to succumb than to reveal the truth straightaway? It was a wretched choice to have to make.

If only he could get his hands on the treasure before they came again. If only he could get away with it and disappear; go to some place where they could never find him.

And where Martine could not come pestering him for money.

Such a sweet dream.

But no more than that.

Yet some dreams came true.

So he had heard.

So maybe.

★   ★   ★

He decided to take another look at the sketch map. And then something struck him that should have been obvious from the start. Those capital letters: D G H and O were each close to a cluster of those little boxes that he had already concluded probably represented four small towns or villages. So what more likely than that the capitals were the initial letters of the places they were close to? Why not, therefore, take another look at his road map and check whether one of the triangles contained four such places whose initials matched up?

Why on earth had he not thought of this before?

He spread out the map and checked all the triangles. Not one of them filled the bill.

Back to square one.

He lit a cigarette and made another check. Same result.

Yet the letters had to be there for a purpose. So what had his brain missed?

Quite by chance his eye was caught by a place marked on his map of the Eastern Counties. The name of it was Exham, and it appeared to be a small village at a corner of one of the triangles. It was in a roughly corresponding position to that of the one in Brogan's sketch marked by the letter D. This was close but not close enough; it should have been E. So no help there. It was so frustrating it nearly made him weep.

The butt of the cigarette was almost burning his lips when he had his next inspiration. Suppose Brogan had been even more ingenious. Suppose he had used the preceding letter in the alphabet, the D, instead of the E, to mark Exham. Then the next village, a place named Inglewood, ought to have the letter H marking it. But it did not; it had G. This stymied Caley for a while, until it occurred to him that Brogan might have increased the back-spacing to two letters in this case. Building on this supposition he made a guess that the next increase would be three letters for a place called Kenthorpe. And sure enough this was marked by the letter H. He was not then surprised to discover that a fourth village, for he had now concluded that they were all villages, was marked O, though the name of it was South Wootton.

So now he had identified all the villages situated in the triangle, and the greatest distance between any two, checked by reference to the scale on his map, was no more than five miles.

Bingo!

Exham, Inglewood, Kenthorpe and South Wootton: these were the four keys to his fortune. All he had to do now was to get himself a spade and drive down into the country, identify the marker trees and dig up his treasure. The digging would have to be done at dead of night of course, but he would need to find the trees in daylight.

No problem.

So once again: Bingo!

There was of course one fly in the ointment. Or rather there were three of them: Josh Tulley, Slim Harker and Lugs Starke. This thought put a check on his feeling of euphoria but did not banish it completely. First things first; and that meant wasting no time in getting down into the identified part of rural England, finding the four villages and the silver birches and unearthing the gold.

He would get cracking on it the very next

day, and it should not take long. Maybe then he would move to some part of the country where the thugs could not find him and he would be free from Martine's importunities. Maybe he could hide the gold and sell it little by little, while living the good life under an assumed name. There were plenty of crooked dealers who would take it from him and ask no questions regarding its origin. They would take a whacking profit of course, but no matter; he would get more than enough for all his needs.

There would be no need to go abroad, which was something that did not appeal to him. He could be perfectly happy in almost any part of his native land as long as he was out of the reach of the erstwhile partners in crime of the late and not wholly lamented Chuck Brogan.

So after all perhaps: Bingo!

15

Cherry

Angela Crowe accompanied Oliver Danby when he went down to the marina at Linburgh to go aboard his yacht. He had picked her up in Norwich before making the journey to the coast, and she would wait until he sailed before taking the Range Rover back to the city, where she would perform her almost non-existent duties at the office until his return.

She had no idea where he was going. Once or twice she had thought of asking the question and then had thought better of it. Some day perhaps he might volunteer the information of his own accord, and then again he might not. She would just have to wait and see.

Cynthia Danby had shown no interest at all in the departure of her husband. She must have returned home at some time during the night but had not made enough noise to awaken him in his separate bedroom. He departed while she was still asleep, feeling no compulsion to rouse her merely in order to tell her he was leaving. He was quite sure that her interest would have been negligible and that she would probably have been annoyed with him for waking her. So he had gone without a parting word or a kiss and had left her to her own devices for an unspecified length of time. Such was the pattern of their lives.

With Miss Crowe it was different.

'I shall miss you,' she said.

Which was the truth.

'And I you.'

Which might have been.

'I'll be counting the days.'

'Do you find that helps the time to pass?'

'No, but I do it all the same. I mark the calendar.'

Danby laughed. 'Well, so do I, if you must know.'

'Well, yes. But for you it's different. Something's happening all the time. At least, I imagine it is.'

'You might be surprised. For quite long periods it can be very boring.'

'Then why — ' she said, and stopped, because she had almost asked a question that might have strayed into forbidden territory.

He answered it anyway, even though it was incomplete.

'Because I must.'

Which was hardly the kind of information to provide her with much enlightenment. But she had expected nothing better. In many respects he was still a mystery to her. Yet in a way this increased rather than diminished the charm of their relationship. She knew that she had been in luck when he had chosen her to work for him — if you could call it work — and if he did not wish to take her completely into his confidence he had a perfect right not to do so. She had no complaints.

She watched until the yacht was out of sight and then returned to the Range Rover. She got in, started the engine and headed back to Norwich.

★　★　★

Osprey was a trim little craft, not many years old and fitted with most of the devices that had made single-handed ocean-going in small boats a much simpler activity than it had been in the days of the early voyagers like Slocombe and Voss. The materials supplied for their use were different too. There were man-made fibres for ropes and sails, giving greater strength and durability, while low-geared winches lent amazing power to a man's hand.

Slocombe designed for his boat an early self-steering device that was crude by modern standards, and navigation had now been simplified by the Satellite Positioning System. Tubular metal alloy masts and booms were lighter and stiffer than those made of wood, and below decks there were instruments unheard of in days gone by. Yet there were still forces of nature to be encountered, and storms could sink a boat or even a mighty ship on the ocean as they had always done.

Danby's yacht was two-masted and ketch-rigged. It was some thirty feet long and ten feet in the beam. A two-cylinder Perkins diesel engine provided auxiliary power if this were needed and the accommodation was comfortable even if a trifle cramped.

In the hands of one experienced sailor, such as Oliver Danby undoubtedly was, *Osprey* was as capable of circumnavigating the globe as Drake's ship, the *Golden Hind*, had been with a full crew of hardy seamen. And perhaps more so.

Not that Danby had any intention of embarking on such an extended voyage. He planned to cross only one ocean — the Atlantic; and to do so by taking the easiest possible route. He proposed therefore to make the voyage in two stages, as he had done on a number of previous occasions. The first stage would take him out of the North Sea, through the English Channel and thence to Tenerife in the Canary Islands.

In Tenerife he would have only a brief stay, during which he would take on fresh fruit and water before setting sail again on the long haul westward.

★　★　★

From the Canaries he made good progress, and after an uneventful voyage during which he sighted few ships, he reached his destination a few weeks later.

Which, he reflected, was just as it should be, but was not always so. He had, however, never had to face any problem at sea that he could not handle, though there was always the possibility of some disaster occurring however much care might be taken. You had to have luck, and so far that was exactly what he had had. He hoped matters would continue thus, for the life such as he was living was a good one, and he did not wish for any change; at least not in the near future. When he grew old, if he ever lived that long, maybe it would all become rather too much for him and he would have to call it a day. But that was still a long way off and he did not dwell on the thought of it. The prospect of Shakespeare's seventh — and last age of man — sans teeth, sans eyes, sans taste, sans everything was a pretty bleak one; and even the sixth was bad enough — the lean and slippered pantaloon, with spectacles on nose and pouch on side, had no appeal for him.

'I'd cut my throat first,' he thought.

But perhaps it would never come to that. Perhaps the great adventure that was life would have for him an abrupt and even violent conclusion long before old age came creeping up on him like a thief in the night. He hoped so. Yes, he really hoped so.

★   ★   ★

The island was one of the Leeward group, part of the Lesser Antilles in the West Indies. It was so small that most people had never heard of it. It's name was Monango, though who had first called it that in the long distant past was a matter for conjecture. Possibly it was the corruption of a name once used only by its native inhabitants, the ill-fated Caribs. Who could tell? Who even cared?

It was, against all the odds, a prosperous island. At least some of its chiefly black inhabitants were; others maybe not. The gap between the haves and the have-nots was as wide on this small fragment of land as it was in just about every other country in the world.

To this island it was that Danby took his yacht at the end of the Atlantic crossing. He discovered, not at all to his surprise, that he was far from being the first to drop anchor in the bay which served as a perfect harbour for small craft, and even for some of much larger size.

It was quite a picture: the blue water of the bay thrusting an arm into the land, a silver beach with a huddle of white-painted houses at the upper edge and beyond these palm trees and verdure-clad hills rising here and there to bare peaks like fingers pointing to the sky.

There were a few wooden jetties jutting out from the inner shore, and these were lined with small boats, while larger ones were lying at anchor in the bay. Of these by far the greater number were power craft; rakish motor-cruisers that looked as if they could manage a pretty useful turn of speed if needed. Danby would have made a bet that almost all of them were American owned, and that the owners were not short of a dollar or two.

In his little yacht he felt like a small boy in a gathering of his elders and superiors when he dropped anchor in their midst. But he cheered himself with the reflection that he had crossed the Atlantic under sail while they had merely steered their engine-driven launches down from Miami or points further north along the eastern seaboard of the United States.

* * *

It was dark when he went ashore in the rubber dinghy, though it was still not much past six o'clock in the evening. He squeezed the dinghy into a narrow gap between two of the boats at one of the jetties and climbed a short flight of steps to the boardwalk. There was a light breeze coming off the sea and he felt pleasantly cool in his khaki shorts and bush jacket. He had canvas shoes on his feet and it was the first touch he had had for weeks of something firm and unmoving under his tread. It felt strange at first, as though in fact the ground were moving and he had to take care to keep his balance.

The sky was cloudless, but the stars were dimmed by the lights of the town, which though small was no doubt the capital of the island and maybe its only port. Its name was St Charles.

There were people moving around, mostly black or brown, but with a sprinkling of whites, probably from the boats out in the bay. One or two of them greeted him as an old acquaintance, and he had indeed been to the island enough times to make himself known around the place.

'Hi, there, Oliver! So you back.'

'Yes, I'm back.'

'Can't stay away, huh?'

'Too true.'

As if drawn by a magnet, he made his way to a bar from which the sound of Caribbean music could be heard. He went inside and saw her there in an instant, though she was at the far end of the long room. She was sitting with a group of white men, Americans for sure, and coloured women. She was facing the door and she must have seen him walk in, for she stood up at once and rushed towards him.

'Olleevah! So you here again.'

She was young and her skin was the colour of milky coffee. She had the kind of figure that men dream about and other women wish they had. She was a beauty, no doubt about it. Danby's heart gave a kick when he saw her, as it always did. Now and then he wondered whether some day he ought to take her away with him, to have her with him for ever and ever. But he knew it would never work out. She would grow older and the beauty would fade, and there would be nothing left.

And besides, there was Angela.

The American she had been sitting with was shouting to make himself heard above the din. He wanted her to come back to where she had been sitting before Danby came in; but she ignored him. Danby took her arm and guided her through the press to the bar. For himself he ordered rum and coke, which he had not tasted for some time. Cherry, for that rather surprisingly, was the girl's name, had Pepsi-Cola with nothing added. Danby had never seen her drink anything alcoholic and he believed she avoided the booze altogether. Which was something else to mark up to her credit.

The American was still showing an inclination to cause trouble, but his companions managed to calm him down. For her part Cherry did not even glance in his direction. She seemed to be indicating that as far as she was concerned he was of the past.

She spoke to Danby. 'I have been waiting for you. Why you take so long to come?'

'It's the way of things.'

'I wish it wasn't.'

'So you miss me, do you?'

She seized his left arm just above the elbow in a surprisingly fierce grip. 'You know I do. I don' live when you not here.'

'And yet,' he said, 'you appear to me to be in the very best of health.'

'Damn you,' she said. 'You mocking me?'

'Never, Cherry, never. I love you too much.'

'Ha!'

It could, he thought, have been an expression of disbelief. It could have been anything.

★　★　★

Later he took her out to *Osprey* in the dinghy. She was to be with him, on board or ashore, for the rest of his stay in that part of the world.

16

Waiting

They were all waiting.

They all knew what they were waiting for but it was never mentioned. It was as though that one subject were taboo. Anything else could be talked about, but not that. And yet it was present at the back of everyone's mind; it was the most important matter they could think about; it was the reason why they were there. It was the reason why other yachts and cruisers arrived and dropped anchor and waited too; counting the days as they passed and maybe impatient to get on with something, and not yet able to.

And all this time there was a stretch of water at the centre of the bay where no boat lay at anchor; as though it had been reserved for some vessel that was not yet there.

★　★　★

Some of the Americans who came ashore looked pretty tough cookies, and Danby suspected that they packed guns. He avoided them. The last thing he wanted was to get himself involved in any kind of fight.

There seemed to be no women on board any of the cruisers and yachts. If there were they must have been keeping themselves out of sight; but he guessed that they were simply not there. The boats were not on a pleasure cruise; they were there for quite a different purpose, and women might have got in the way.

He had heard that on one of the boats, and perhaps even more than one, gambling sessions were taking place. He himself had been invited to take part, but had declined. He was no dab hand at poker and he never gambled except occasionally on the gee-gees; and then only in moderation. He would have been a fool to lose all his money on a throw of the cards when he would so soon be needing it. He had seen a couple of the boats haul up anchor and leave the bay, and he could imagine the fury of their owners who lost far more than their stake money at the card table.

For himself there were more enjoyable things to do. Like lying naked in a narrow bunk with a naked brown-skinned girl entwining her dream of a body with his. Why would he need the excitement of pasteboard kings and queens and knaves when he had something so much better calculated to set the blood coursing through his veins?

The fact was that he for one did not find time hanging like a dead weight on his hands. He did not gaze at first light towards the entrance to the bay and at the stretch of salt water beyond, cursing again when nothing met the eye except the seabirds and the distant horizon.

★ ★ ★

Some days they lay on the beach or swam in the almost tepid water of the bay. Sometimes they did a little fishing; and if they caught anything Cherry would cook it in the tiny galley.

'When,' she said, 'are you going to take me to England?'

'Some day. Not yet.'

'You promised.'

This was true. In a moment of weakness after they had been making ecstatic love he had said he would take her back with him. At that moment he would have promised her the world. Later, of course, the absurdity of it struck him. Take her to England; introduce her to Cynthia and Angela?

'This is my wife. And this is my girlfriend.'

'Why are you laughing?' she demanded. 'Is it a joke?'

'No joke,' he said. 'I laugh when I'm happy.'

'And what makes you happy now?'

'The thought of you in England with me.'

'You like that?'

'I like it very much.'

'But not yet?'

'No, not yet.'

She frowned. 'So when?'

'Soon, maybe.'

'Only maybe?'

'Nobody can see into the future,' Danby said. 'You have to take things as they come and make the best of them.'

He could see that it did not satisfy her. She seemed quite put out for a time. But soon her normal high spirits took over again and the question of when he would be taking her to England was pushed into the background.

★ ★ ★

One day he rented a car from a garage in St Charles. It was a not very new Ford convertible which he drove with the hood down. There was a road like a switchback that girdled the island, almost touching the coast in places and in others turning inland as if to pay a call on some tiny village nestling in the hills. It was a green island; everything seemed to grow freely.

In many places there were crops of a tall plant like a kind of grass, which he did not recognise.

'What is that?' he asked.

Cherry smiled. 'Ganja.'

'Ganja?'

'Hemp, hashish, pot, marijuana. You name it.'

'So they grow it here?'

'Sure. Had to. Used to be bananas. Then big Yankee firms grow them cheaper in Central America and kill the banana trade. So people turn to this instead. Make more profit.'

'So where do they sell it?'

'Where you think? The biggest market.'

'You mean the United States?'

'Where else?'

Danby laughed. 'So some of your people get their own back in that way?'

'You bet. Why not? Gotta look after yourself. Nobody else will. Least of all big brother up north.'

'That's true.'

And was it not what he too was doing? One way and another. Looking after number one and to hell with the rest.

★　★　★

He stayed two weeks. That was the length of time which elapsed before the ship arrived. It came with the first light and moved into the space reserved for it at the centre of the bay. The anchor went down with a rattle in a cloud of red rust and dried mud, and the ship came to rest.

Cherry was still asleep, but he woke her.

'She's here.'

She blinked at him. 'Who?'

'The ship.'

The news was hardly calculated to send her into raptures of delight; and it did not.

'You wake me up to tell me that?'

'You don't sound happy.'

'Why would I be? It mean you be leaving soon now.'

'Well, yes, but — '

'And you think that make me happy?'

He had no answer to that, so he went back on deck and took another look at the ship. It was not big; maybe a three thousand tonner. And it was old. It was rusty and dirty and it was sailing under a flag of covenience. With the aid of binoculars he could make out the name on the bows: *Horace G Gardener*, port of registration Monrovia. It was about what he would have expected. And he would have hazarded a guess that the crew matched the vessel. None of this worried him. He would not be sailing in the *Horace G*. He would never set foot on her filthy decks. She was important to him simply because of what she had brought to the island.

He went below again and found that Cherry was up and had started preparing breakfast. She seemed to have regained her usual cheerfulness even though she knew that the arrival of the ship signalled the imminent departure of her lover. She lived in the hope, and indeed the expectation that perhaps sooner than later he would fulfil his promise to take her to England with him.

'When will you go ashore?' she asked.

'Oh, not for a while yet. There's no need to hurry. I'll wait until the rush is over.'

'You're not afraid there won't be enough to go round?'

'It's never been a problem in the past. A ship that size could really carry a load of the stuff and hardly notice it.'

'Same one, is it?'

'Oh, yes. Maybe they have the contract.'

'How much you think they get paid?'

'I've no idea. Plenty, I guess.'

'Everybody gets his cut. Is that it?'

'That's it. It's the way the world goes round.'

She looked thoughtful. Then, as if it had

only just occurred to her: 'It's dirty though, isn't it?'

He sensed a criticism of himself, and he resented it. 'So is arms dealing. And a lot of other trades. Nothing is really clean when you look into it closely.'

'Um!' she said. And he could tell she did not believe him.

He did not believe it himself. It was too sweeping. It was the sort of thing you said when you felt you were in a corner. She had raised a question he did not wish to look at too closely, and for a moment she had had him on the ropes.

17

Business

It was evening when he went ashore. He had left Cherry on board, because he was going on business and she had no part of it.

The room was on the first floor of a house on the far side of the town; a clapboard building with no pretensions to style. He guessed there had been a steady stream of visitors coming to this room all day and departing within a short space of time, their business done. He had noticed how the boats in the bay had thinned out; one after another with anchors hauled up heading for the open sea. *Osprey* might well be the last to leave, and that not until the next day. He was in no hurry. What was one day more or less when you had an ocean to cross?

There was a landing at the top of a flight of bare wooden stairs, and on the right was a door standing slightly ajar. He gave a knock and walked in without waiting for an invitation. He was the customer and he felt no obligation to stand on ceremony. He was carrying a canvas kitbag, but there was no kit in it; just a bundle of paper money; quite a lot of it brought all the way from the United Kingdom.

There were four men in the room and they were all smoking. Two had cigarettes and the other two were chewing on fat cigars. A window was open but it was hot nevertheless, and the air was scarcely fit to breathe because of the smoke.

Two of the men were white, or nearly so. They were heavily built and had coarse black hair and big moustaches, swarthy complexions and plenty of dark stubble on cheeks and chins. They were toting guns and probably would not have been slow to use them if the occasion arose.

Danby knew they were Colombians and he decided not to do anything that might have been calculated to make it arise.

The other two were blacks, natives of the island, and he had had dealings with them before. One was Joe and the other was Sam. He had never had any trouble with them and he expected none now.

'Hi there, Oliver,' Joe said. 'You late again.'

'Not too late, I hope.'

'No chance. Never too late for business.'

There was a table in the room. It looked heavy and strong enough to bear the weight of several men, if any men wanted to stand on it. On the table was an old-fasioned weighing-machine with brass weights.

'How much you want this time?' Sam asked.

Danby tipped the contents of the kitbag onto the table. There were dollar bills of various denominations but all of the higher values. A lot of them.

'That much.'

It was the blacks who counted them. The two Colombians appeared to have a watching brief. They just chewed their cigars and looked on. But Danby would have made a guess that they were missing nothing.

The merchandise, which was cocaine, was in polythene bags. It was weighed out and handed over to Danby, who stowed it in the kitbag. It made quite a bulge when it was all in. He slung it on his shoulder and walked to the door.

'When you come again?' Joe asked.

'Who knows?' Danby said. 'There's a lot of ocean to cross both ways.'

'Sooner you than me in that li'l boat.'

'Somebody has to do it,' Danby said.

They both laughed at that. It seemed to amuse them, this suggestion that he might be performing a public service. The Colombians had said nothing all through the transaction. They had just stood aside, smoking their cigars and looking sinister. Danby was glad to get them out of his sight.

★ ★ ★

'So,' Cherry said, 'you won't be leaving tonight?'

'I never start a voyage after dark,' Danby said.

'And you're not going to take me with you?'

'Not this time, sweetheart. Don't be impatient. There's a good time coming.'

'Maybe. But when?'

'Soon.'

'That a promise?'

'It's a promise.'

And perhaps he would keep the promise; perhaps he would take her to England and set her up in a smart London hotel. It would make an interesting situation and would delight the girl. But then there would be no one to welcome him at this end of the line; for there was certainly not another like her in St Charles.

So on second thoughts maybe it was not such a hot idea after all. It would cause too many complications, and there were enough of them already.

★ ★ ★

The last of the American boats had gone before he set sail. Soon they would be off the coast of Florida or Georgia and the cocaine would be leaking ashore. These boats were hardly ever caught as their owners carried on this lucrative trade. They were fast, high-powered craft and could leave a Coast Guard cutter struggling to keep in touch.

So the drug came pouring in through innumerable gaps in the defences. And it was brought not only by sea but also overland across the Mexican border or by the plane load direct from Colombia to isolated airfields here and there in Texas or other southern states.

Compared with all this Danby's little bag of the drug seemed paltry. But paltry or not, it enabled him to live the good life and never go short of anything he might desire. And for his part there was no dodging of the American Coast Guard to be done, because his voyages never took him into the territorial waters of the United States. When he set sail from St Charles he was far to the south of that danger area, and soon he was away to the east of it as well.

He himself never used the stuff in any of its forms. He eschewed the commodity from which he drew his wealth and all other addictive drugs as well. He regarded drug-taking, whether you snorted it or breathed it into your lungs as smoke or injected it into your bloodstream with a needle, as a mug's game. Nevertheless, he was perfectly willing to make his fortune from the weakness of those mugs.

Though of course he himself never went near them, the ultimate users of that commodity which originated as the leaf of a small bush in the interior of Colombia. He was never there on the streets pushing the stuff; he was not even one of those who supplied the pushers. He was further back in the supply line and could almost kid himself that his hands were clean.

And after all, did he not, time and again, risk his life on the high seas in a small boat that might sometime or other be over-whelmed and sunk by a sudden storm or a freak tidal wave?

So one way or another he managed to persuade himself that there was nothing really wrong with what he was doing. And even if there had been he would still have done it, because, damn it all, you had to make a living somehow in this cut-throat world of devil-take-the-hindmost. Like it or not, that was the way things were; and he had not set the standard.

'So now,' Cherry said, 'you going back to that great big house of yours. Tell me 'bout it.'

'I have told you.'

'Tell me again.'

So he told her again. And the way he told it made his property sound like some grand country mansion, maybe centuries old, and not just a fairly new five-bedroom dwelling with every modern convenience; warm and comfortable but with no pretensions to architectural distinction. Sometimes he felt a touch of guilt at deceiving her. But he could see that it pleased her, so what harm was there in this innocent deception? After all, she would never be disillusioned by a sight of his real mansion in a far off country.

★ ★ ★

He had to take her ashore in the dinghy before he sailed. It was an odd thing, but he had never seen where she lived when he was not there. She had never spoken about it, nor much about herself. He supposed there was a family of some kind in the background, but he had never met any of them, and of what she did with herself when he was not there he had no idea. He asked no questions because he did not really wish to know the answers. Some of the magic of her might have been lost for him if he had peered too deeply into the secret of that life she lived apart from him. It was better this way.

★ ★ ★

He used the diesel engine to propel *Osprey* clear of the bay. Then he cut the motor and hoisted sail. When he looked back he could see her still there, watching from the shore. He waved to her, but she did not wave back, and after a while she had vanished from his sight.

Though neither of them could have guessed it at the time, they were destined never to see each other again.

18

Kimberley

The gang of three, Josh Tulley, Slim Harker and Lugs Starke, had a girl living with them. She was an eighteen-year-old prostitute named Kimberley, or Kim for short. She had never told them what her surname was and they never asked. It was of no importance.

She had run away from her home in the Midlands at the age of sixteen because her father had raped her twice and her mother refused to believe her. She had gravitated inevitably to London and had fallen into the ready hands of a pimp named Lammy Buller. He was called Lammy because he was fond of lamming people, especially those who were unable to lam him back, like the girls he managed. He was a nasty piece of work whichever way you looked at him, and it was a great mystery to all who knew him why he had never landed up in jail. If anyone deserved to be there, he was the one.

It was Tulley who brought Kimberley back to the run-down old house where they were living, and they all liked the look of her;

which was hardly surprising because she was a really attractive blonde. No doubt this was why Lammy had got his fangs into her in the first place, because he had an eye for that sort of thing.

There was one blemish on her appearance when Tulley brought her in. It was a rather nasty bruise on her left temple which was not completely masked by the long blonde hair.

'Howjer get that?' Harker asked.

She answered with one word: 'Lammy.'

'He bin knocking you about?'

'What you think? He knocks us all about. He enjoys it. He's a sadist.'

Harker was not sure what a sadist was, but he guessed it was something bad.

'Wotcher mean — all?'

'Well, there's three other girls, you know.'

Harker sucked his teeth. 'Ah! A right little stable.'

She told them the others were foreigners — two Romanian and one Albanian from Kosovo.

'I believe he bought them.'

'Like they was slaves,' Tulley said.

'That's about it.'

'So he knocks them about too?'

'Yes. Whenever he feels like it. Which is often.'

'So why don't they just walk out on him?'

'They wouldn't dare. They're illegal immigrants, smuggled into the country in the back of a lorry or something. He's threatened to go to the coppers and tell on them if they don't toe the line.'

'He never would, you know. He'd as soon throw hisself off Tower Bridge as go near the Old Bill.'

'Well, maybe so. But how are they to know that?'

'Still and all,' Tulley said, 'that's no reason why you should stick with him. You ain't an illegal immigrant. So why don't you leave him? Get to hell out of it. I reckon he takes most what you earn, the lousy bastard.'

'That's true.'

'So why not do it? Give him the two fingers and get to hell out.'

'But where would I go?'

Tulley looked at the other two and seemed to have an idea. It was such a good idea it made him laugh.

'Well, why don't you come here with us? Plenty spare room.'

She looked at him doubtfully, as if she thought he might be kidding. 'You mean come and live with you lot?'

Tulley cast another look at Harker and Starke. 'Wotcher say, lads? You think we might give the little lady house room?'

When it dawned on them what he was suggesting there was hardly any hesitation. The prospect of having a resident whore in the house seemed almost too good to be true. And not just any old faggot but one as young and pretty as this. So they gave the thumbs up and for their part the deal was done.

Kim hesitated scarcely longer than they had. It could hardly have been said that three crooks like these, a great deal older than she was and no beauties with the possible exception of Starke, would have had much allure as prospective housemates, but when the alternative was continued working for a swine like Lammy Buller who took most of what you earned and beat you up whenever he felt like it, the whole thing took on a different aspect.

'You're serious, are you? Not just having me on.'

'Why would we do that?' Tulley asked. 'Where would it get us?'

And Harker said: 'Too true, we're serious. You can trust us kid. Sure you can.'

Which was about the most unlikely statement he could have made.

She seemed to think about it; but only for a few moments. Then: 'Well, if you're really sure — '

'You bet we're sure,' Starke said.

And that made three of them signalling approval of the move, and the deed was done.

★ ★ ★

She fetched her things later that day. They did not amount to much and were all contained in one fairly large shoulderbag.

'Looks like you ain't bin feathering your nest very much,' Tulley said. 'That all you got?'

'Yeah.'

'Lammy bin taking a helluva big whack from your earnings, I reckon.'

'That's true.'

'What'd he say when you told him you was clearing out? Giving him the old heave-ho?'

'Nothing.'

'He didn't object? How come?'

'I didn't tell him. He can just find out for himself.'

'He won't like it.'

'No, he won't, will he?' She sounded just a shade worried, as though thinking of possible repercussions. But then she said: 'Still, what can he do?'

'Nothing, if you stay clear of him.'

'Oh, I'll do that. Betcha life, I will.'

★ ★ ★

She settled in pretty quickly and seemed pleased with her new quarters; which might have been taken as an indication of how rough the previous ones had been. She did a little cleaning-up and a bit of cooking; but she was not in the top rank at either activity.

She was still plying her old trade, which was reputed to be the oldest profession in the world; but she had prudently shifted her operations to a different area in order to avoid any probable contact with Lammy. She was still afraid of him; and though there were three pretty tough characters to protect her, they could not be with her when she was out and about. So it was as well for her to take care.

In theory the arrangement between the four occupants of the house had been that they should pool their resources; but for a start at least the men's contribution to expenses had been low because they had been having a lean time recently and living more or less from hand to mouth. So it turned out that Kimberley became the chief bread winner and poured the greater part of her earnings into the common pool.

Not that this appeared to bother her at all. Apparently she was perfectly content to keep for herself only a small part of what came to her from the punters. It was, she said, more than Lammy had ever let her hold back for her own disposal; so she was better off anyway.

'I'm happy,' she said, 'If you are.'

And of course none of them saw any reason to be unhappy. She was a pretty good earner and her arrival on the scene was the best thing that had happened to them for quite some time.

To encourage her to stay Tulley explained to her that, though they were a trifle pushed for the ready just then, it would not always be like that. They were certain that something big would turn up in the near future. And he did mean big, really big. He did not tell her what it was; he thought it was wiser to leave her in the dark on that point. She might have kept the information to herself, but on the other hand she might not, and there was no point in taking the risk of her maybe blabbing about it to one of her clients. What she didn't know she couldn't reveal; and that was the way it had better be.

What he did tell her was that when the day came they would all be rich.

'Stinking rich. You included.'

'You mean you're going to share it with me? Whatever it is.'

'Sure. Why not? You're one of us now and there'll be enough.' He glanced at Harker and

Starke. 'That's right, ain't it?'

'Reckon so,' Starke said. But he did not seem so sure. 'Though she don't get as much as us.'

'Well, no,' Tulley agreed. 'Pro rata, pro rata.'

He was not sure precisely what that meant, but it sounded right.

'I don't want any,' Kim said. 'Living here's enough for me.'

'You'll change your mind when you see what it is,' Tulley said. 'It'll mean no more hanging around street corners on freezing cold nights with the wind blowing up your skirt. You'll be able to say goodbye to all that.'

She had to admit that this would be a good thing, but he could tell that she was taking it all as so much pie in the sky and not banking on it.

* ★ ★

They had decided that there need be no hurry to get the information they wanted from Caley. It was Tulley's suggestion that they should give him a bit more time.

'Maybe he'll locate the stuff for us if he got information from Chuck. Which I reckon he must have. We could let him dig it up and then move in and take it off him.'

'You think it's buried then?' Starke said.

'Seems likely. If he'd hid it anyhow else somebody would have stumbled on it by now. Yes, you can be sure he put it underground. He had a spade in that van of his. Afraid he might get stuck sometime and need it.'

'And you still believe he told Caley where to find it?'

'Must have. No other reason why he'd give the guy a free meal. He wasn't all that generous.'

'So for the present we just hang around and keep our eyes skinned for any move our friend may make.'

'That's the ticket. But we gotta watch our step. We don't wanter make the filth suspicious.'

'They're suspicious anyway.'

'True enough. But they ain't got nothing concrete to work on. So they're stuck. That guy Caley musta made them hopping mad when he didn't pick out me and Slim in the line-up,' Tulley said. 'And that's another thing points to him having some information we ain't got.'

It was Harker who remarked that they were lucky to have Kimberley bringing in money for their expenses.

'We'd be really pushed else.'

'Well,' Tulley said, 'she's getting something

in return. She's got a roof over her head and she ain't being knocked around by that bastard, Lammy Buller.'

'All the same,' Harker said, 'you can't say as we got the sticky end of the bargain.'

They all had a bit of a laugh at that, thinking of the nice little blonde who was even then somewhere out in the night air earning the cash that kept the ménage going.

'She's a real sweetie,' Harker said.

And that was a point on which they were all agreed. Kimberley really was a sweetie.

And she was theirs.

19

Excursion for Caley

Caley set out early in the morning. It was a wretched day, and if he had been a believer in omens he might have rated this as one of the worst. It rained all the way. Sometimes it was heavy, sometimes light; but, heavy or light, it never completely left off. He had to keep the windscreen wipers in the pick-up truck going all the time.

But by eight o'clock he was clear of the London sprawl and was on the M11 heading in the direction of Cambridge. He was a careful, and indeed a somewhat nervous driver. Driving was something he did from necessity rather than for pleasure. He never drove very fast, and other vehicles were forever overtaking him. For quite a while he was stuck behind a monstrous juggernaut of a lorry which seemed to be a mile long and which he had not the courage to overtake. Fortunately he lost it when he left the M11 and got himself on the road to Newmarket, though the continuing rain made the prospect a dismal one. If it had not been for the conviction that he was bound to discover the whereabouts of a cache of gold at the end of his journey he might have been in a very depressed state of mind indeed. But even low cloud, rain and the nervous strain of driving in traffic could not succeed in banishing that rosy vision from his head.

'Soon now,' he muttered. 'Very soon now and you'll be rich.'

He had no doubt whatever that his final interpretation of Chuck Brogan's rough sketch map had been the correct one and that it would be a simple matter to identify the three silver birches that marked the site of the cache.

There was a brand new spade in the back of the truck and a canvas tilt which would be used to conceal the gold bars when he had dug them up. He had not yet made up his mind whether he would carry out the disinterment that night or leave it until later when he had worked out exactly what the next step was to be. He must not be too hasty; he had to think of all eventualities and guard against anything that might conceivably go wrong.

His chief worries were two in number: the police and the gang of three. With the gold in his possession it was imperative that he avoid both the law-enforcers and the law-breakers.

So would it be wise to take the gold to his place at all? There, if only for a day or a night, it would be vulnerable. A sudden unforeseen raid at the critical moment, and all could be lost. Indeed, it might be a wiser course when he had the treasure dug up to head at once for some other part of the country and never again return to his place in Canning Town.

When he had reached this point in his reasoning he saw plainly that it would indeed be foolish to start digging without delay. In any case it would have to be done at night — and very late at night too — since the activity would be bound to raise suspicions in the mind of anyone catching sight of it; especially if that someone happened to be a policeman. The map gave no indication of the distance of the trees from the road, though it was unlikely to be very great, since bars of gold were, he imagined, pretty heavy, and Chuck would have had to carry them one by one from his van to the burial place.

Another reason for postponing the digging, even after the site had been identified, was that if he were to do as he had now decided would be best — which was to take the gold hoard immediately to a far safer part of the country than Canning Town — he would need to pack some luggage before making his final departure.

'Of course!'

He took one hand off the steering wheel and gave himself a smack on the forehead. How could he have been so stupid as not to have thought of that before? A man setting off to a new life in some distant region did not depart with just the clothes he stood up in even if he was taking a load of precious metal with him. He packed a bag, a suitcase, maybe two or three suitcases, as much as he could carry.

So why had not this occurred to him at once? Was he so lacking in commonsense as not to see that operations like this needed more planning than he had carried out? Well, he had thought of everything now — at least he hoped he had — and the immediate task was to find those four East Anglian villages in their triangle of roads.

As far as he could judge from his map, that part of Norfolk he was looking for was somewhere to the east of the A11 before this road came to Norwich; and at a small town called Attleborough, some ten miles from the city, he took a turning to the right and got the pick-up onto some minor roads which he found about as difficult to navigate as the maze at Hampton Court. There were signposts here and there, but these could be misleading. Some had been vandalised so that the arms pointed in wrong directions, while others had no arms at all. On one occasion the road he had been following took him to a farmyard, and he was forced to reverse the truck and beat a hasty retreat.

He imagined he was progressing in more or less the right direction, but what with the rain and the murk and his own lack of navigational skill, he could not be at all certain. What he was sure of was that nowhere had he seen a signpost directing him to any village with the name of one or other of the four he was seeking. It was as if they did not exist.

It was getting on for midday when he came to another that was not one of those he was looking for; but it had a public house called The Fox and he decided to ask inside for directions that might help him in his quest. So he took the truck onto a shingle forecourt and went inside.

It was the kind of village pub of which there remained a steadily diminishing number, and there were three elderly customers sitting on a high-backed bench in the bar. They all turned their gaze on Caley when he entered, as if he had been a creature from outer space, but they said nothing.

There was no one behind the bar, but there

was a bell, and when Caley had rung it a man appeared from somewhere, sleeves rolled up to the elbow and wearing a white apron. He was middle-aged, rather stout and bald-headed. He enquired what he could do for Caley, who ordered half a pint of bitter. It was then that he became aware of signals from his stomach that an offering of food would be appreciated. He had eaten nothing since breakfast and he was hungry.

Fortunately, The Fox was equipped in the background with a microwave oven, and a half-decent hot meal was quickly prepared. While it was being got ready he asked if there was a village named Kenthorpe anywhere near, and if so how he could best get to it.

The landlord stroked his chin. 'Kenthorpe, hey? Well now, thass about ten mile from here, I'd say.'

One of the elderly men chipped in then. 'More like twelve.'

This started a general argument, which Caley ended by explaining that he was not so much interested in the exact distance as in the way of getting there.

In answer to this question too there seemed to be more than one opinion. But finally the landlord found a sheet of notepaper and a pencil and drew a rough map that was rather better than the one that Brogan had given

Caley, but not much. He accepted it, however, and having finished and paid for his meal he went back to the truck and set out once more in the still-falling rain.

It was an hour later when he came, not to Kenthorpe, but to the place called Inglewood. He breathed a sigh of relief, for he had almost given up hope of finding any of the objects of his search.

What he had at last discovered was a typical Norfolk village of the present day: a number of dwellings, some old, some new, a flint church with a square tower, a graveyard with a number of headstones standing like drunkards at all angles, no pub, no post office, no shop, cars parked here and there, a tractor rumbling through and hauling a trailer loaded with horse manure . . .

What pleased Caley most was a signpost, one arm of which bore the information: SOUTH WOOTTON 5 MILES. And beneath it: KENTHORPE 3 MILES. In spite of the rain his spirits rose at once. He was on the track of the gold bullion at last.

★ ★ ★

On Brogan's map the three silver birches and the cross marking, so he had concluded, the spot where the treasure was buried were fairly close to the village of Kenthorpe, which was apparently situated between Inglewood and South Wootton. So, with steadily rising excitement, he got the truck moving again and headed down the narrow, winding country road that he hoped was destined to lead him to his El Dorado.

It took him very little time to reach Kenthorpe, which was in essentials not greatly different from the village he had just left. There was a church and a number of houses and cottages, some with front doors opening directly onto the road, others with small gardens, mostly used as parking lots for cars. A few of the cottages looked as though they might have been models for paintings by Constable or artists of the Norwich School; but there were some far more modern properties of the kind that might set you back a quarter or even half a million smackers if you had that kind of money to throw around.

Caley drove on through this village, and he was keeping an eye open for any silver birches, but he could see none. In fact, where he had imagined the three markers might have been there was just a large meadow with horses grazing on the short grass. There were no trees of any description.

His spirits sank. A moment or two earlier he had been fully convinced that he had found the object of his search, but now he realised that he had been mistaken. It was heartbreaking.

He had one hope left. Perhaps somehow or other he had read Brogan's sketch map incorrectly, had made a mistake in his working out of the cryptic signs. Perhaps he had pinpointed the wrong spot or the wrong section of the triangle.

He had stopped the truck. Now he started it again and made a tour of those roads that connected the four villages. The total distance was some twelve miles, and he drove slowly, peering through the rain that was still falling and scrutinising the land on each side of the road. Nowhere was there a single silver birch tree, let alone a group of three.

His excursion into the country had been a futile exercise. It had all been in vain.

He was back where he had started.

★   ★   ★

He drove back to London in a mood of deepest depression, not helped by the fact that he lost his way in trying to find the A11. Attleborough seemed to have vanished, and it was not until he had found his way, more or less by accident, to Thetford that he got himself headed in the right direction.

Now, as if to mock him, the rain stopped and the sun came out. It was a beautiful evening, but he was unable to appreciate the beauty. He had set out in the morning with such high hopes. He was returning in the evening with those hopes dashed and a bleak future stretching out before him.

Would he really have to sell his property and start looking for a job? He detested the thought.

And how about those three gangsters? They would soon be starting on him again, believing he had the secret to the whereabouts of the gold. And the irony of it was that, though he had denied it vehemently, he had at that time believed himself in possession of the vital information that would lead him to it. Now it looked as if he had been kidding himself and that he had been telling the plain truth after all.

But if they came after him again, would he be able to convince them that he was no nearer locating the stuff than they were? Even if he showed them Brogan's map as proof that he was indeed telling the truth, would that help? Whether they believed him or not, would they not beat him up for holding out on them at the start? Would they not take out their feelings of frustration on him?

He felt that it was all too likely that they would.

★ ★ ★

And there was Martine too. She would soon be on at him again, nagging, demanding more money. Money, money, money! It was all she thought of. Well, maybe it was all he thought of too, now that it was draining away so fast and the one hope of replenishing the coffers had disappeared on a wet afternoon in the bloody country. He had never been a country-lover, but now he hated it more than ever. For him it was the pits.

★ ★ ★

There was an envelope lying on the mat when he walked into the house in Canning Town. He took it into the office and slit it open. Inside was an offer from some financial institution with a name he had never heard of to lend him any amount of money. He was about to throw it into the wastepaper basket, but stopped.

He lit a cigarette and began to study the offer.

20

Homecoming

Oliver Danby brought his yacht *Osprey* to a stop close in to the shore and let the anchor drop from the bows. It was a still, warm night with just a sliver of moon dodging in and out of the feathery clouds.

Osprey was showing no light; which was a risk that Danby had to take in preference to the other risk of having the yacht's presence revealed to any observer on shore or in a boat.

The yacht had made an uneventful crossing of the Atlantic, and had sailed up the English Channel almost as far as St Alban's head before doubling back under cover of darkness with sails furled and the engine going. It was now somewhat to the west of Lulworth Cove, and Danby was ready to go ashore.

He went in the dinghy, paddling, making little sound. The kitbag containing the parcels of cocaine was in the dinghy with him, and there was also a small shovel with a short handle. Danby was a cool customer, but he always felt his heart beat a little faster at this stage of the operation, because this was when there was most danger. It could never be rated as an impossibility that when he stepped ashore there would be a customs officer waiting for him. It had not happened yet, but this did not guarantee that it never would. And if it did it would be goodbye to so many things that made life pleasant for him. Like the comfortable house in the country, the fictitious export-import business with the office in Norwich and the lovely Miss Crowe looking after it, and the delightful Cherry far across the bright blue sea. All these would be gone in one fell stroke, and with them his freedom, that most precious of all his possessions.

So maybe soon he should call it a day and not push his luck too far. He was living it up right now, but he was still putting one hell of a lot away for the future. Maybe soon there would be enough. Yes, but how soon? That was the question.

And how much was ever enough? That also was a question. And he did not know the answer to either of them.

* * *

He felt the dinghy touch bottom. There was a little surf like a ghostly presence along the shore, but the waves were mere ripples that made no more than a faint hissing sound as they rolled over on the beach. He had been fortunate with the weather all the way on this trip. Sometimes, on his return, he had been obliged to wait far too long before the Channel was calm enough for him to take the dinghy to the beach. He avoided the worst months of the year, but there was enough profit from the trips he did make to provide plenty of the necessary. Oh yes; he was doing very nicely; very nicely indeed.

But how much further ought he to push his luck?

* * *

He stepped out of the dinghy and pulled it clear of the surf. He picked up the kitbag and the shovel and made his way towards the cliff which was outlined as a dark, looming mass silhouetted against the night sky. He had a small torch in the pocket of his windcheater, but this would be used only in an emergency. He knew this part of the shore so well that he could find his way in almost complete darkness. He was wearing shorts and sneakers, with no socks, and his feet made a faint crunching sound as he walked.

He came to the cliff and moved to his left.

Twenty paces took him to the cave he was seeking. It was so low that he had to stoop to get into it, but it went in for several yards. He moved forward in the darkness without switching on the torch and groped his way round a bend to the right. Here he set down the kitbag and began to dig.

The floor was of sand, soft and easy to excavate, and it took him little time to dig a shallow hole large enough to accommodate the kitbag. He rammed it down firmly and covered it with a layer of sand which he smoothed out with a small brush he had brought for the purpose.

He used the torch only momentarily to make sure that his task had been finished thoroughly, and then retreated from the cave, obliterating all evidence that he had been there as he withdrew.

There was always the possibility of course that someone might venture into the cave and start digging around and uncover the kitbag with its highly valuable contents. But this was a risk that had to be taken; and so far there had been no complication of this kind and he thought it unlikely that there ever would be.

He obliterated his footmarks in the vicinity of the cave entrance and returned to the dinghy and paddled back to the waiting yacht. Five minutes later he had hauled up the anchor and was heading eastward up the Channel.

★　★　★

It was a few days after this when the yacht *Osprey* arrived unostentatiously at her berth in the Linburgh marina. It was just eleven o'clock in the morning of a fine bright day, and Danby wasted no time in putting through a telephone call to Angela Crowe, requesting her to bring the Range Rover, because he was home again.

She received the news of his return with undisguised delight, as though she had been looking forward with impatience to nothing else throughout the entire period of his absence.

'Oh, marvellous. How are you?'

'I'm fine. Never better.'

'Lovely. I'll be on my way then.'

'I'll be expecting you.'

He rang off and reflected that it was certainly nice to have someone like the charming Miss Crowe waiting for you at the end of a long voyage; someone who was genuinely delighted to welcome you back. He could be quite certain that his reception when he put in an appearance at the house in Norfolk would not be so effusive.

The formalities of his return to what he was in the habit of referring to as his home port were few. There was no customs office in Linburgh; but on certain occasions in the past officers in that service had stepped on board almost as soon as he arrived. He guessed that somehow they had been fed information regarding the long sea voyages which he made on a fairly regular basis, and being suspicious by nature and training, they had scented a possible smuggling racket. It was of course their duty to sniff out such illegal enterprises and arrest those who might be profiting by them.

So these officers stepped down into the cockpit and proceeded to search the yacht from stem to stern. They went over it with a fine-toothed comb, as it were. But the search produced nothing in the contraband line and they went away empty-handed and not a little disappointed. Latterly he had been free from their attentions, though he knew that they had not given up and might return unexpectedly if the spirit moved them.

Not that this possibility troubled him. On arrival at the marina the yacht was always clean, and he had nothing to declare except possibly a bottle or two of rum.

When Angela arrived in the Range Rover he was ready to leave with a bag already packed. He let her do the driving to Norwich while he relaxed in the passenger seat.

'How have you been amusing yourself since I've been away?' he asked.

She gave a laugh. 'You should know. I've been looking after the shop, haven't I? Like I always do.'

'Many customers?'

'You bet. I've imported and exported loads.'

'That's my girl.'

★　★　★

They went first to the office and made love on the sofa in the small room where this activity regularly took place when Danby was not away on his travels.

Later, with glasses in their hands, he with one of whisky and she with her usual gin and tonic, she said:

'I suppose you're not going to tell me where you've been and what you've been doing?'

He shook his head. 'You wouldn't be interested.'

Which he knew was not the truth. She would most certainly have been interested, especially if he told her about a young brown-skinned girl named Cherry. But he

179

would have been a fool to do that, and no one had ever had reason to call Oliver Danby that.

'And how long will you be here this time?'

'A while.'

Which was not telling her much.

'Sometimes,' she said, 'I think you do it on purpose to tease me.'

'Do what?'

'Make a mystery of yourself. Do you tell other people any more than you tell me?'

'Not a word,' he said. And laughed.

★ ★ ★

When they had showered and dressed they went for a meal at a restaurant and then to a film which Angela said she would like to see. Danby was not much of a filmgoer but he went to please her on this first evening back in England.

★ ★ ★

It was late when he walked into the house, but Cynthia was there. She had been watching some kind of entertainment on television, but she switched it off when he walked in. She greeted him with less effusion than Miss Crowe had shown; indeed, with no effusion at all.

'So you're home.'

'Looks like it, doesn't it?'

'You didn't think it necessary to let me know you were in the country, I suppose.'

'If I had, what would you have done? Rolled out the red carpet?'

She made no answer to that.

Danby sank into an armchair and took a long hard look at his wife. She became uncomfortable under his gaze and turned to face him more squarely.

'Why are you looking at me like that?'

'Like what?'

'As if — oh, I don't know — as if you were weighing me up?'

'Was I really doing that? Well, perhaps I was — in a way. I sometimes wonder, you know, why we go on like this. Why we don't split up. Can it be because in our secret hearts we really adore each other?'

'Don't be an idiot,' she said, rather crossly. 'You know perfectly well why we stick together. Because it suits us both to go on in this way. We each do whatever it is we wish to do and ask no questions regarding the other's activities. What better arrangement could there be?'

'It doesn't ever occur to you that it's a rather one-sided bargain?'

She lifted an eyebrow. 'In what way?'

'Well,' he said, 'I can see how it benefits you. I supply you with everything — cash, car, a roof over your head and so on. But what do I get in return? Tell me that.'

She appeared to give the question some thought. Then: 'Respectability, perhaps.'

He gave a laugh. 'Oh, my dear! What curiously old-fashioned ideas you have to be sure. Positively Victorian. You can't really mean that. Not in this day and age. People don't think in that way any more. Nowadays you behave as you damn well please.'

'So you're grudging me what I cost. Is that it?'

'No,' he said. 'It's not that.'

'What then?'

He shrugged. 'Oh, nothing, nothing. Forget it.'

It was a kind of inertia on his part that kept things as they were. He just could not be bothered to change an arrangement that seemed to work well enough. For the present at least. What the future might hold in store no one could foresee, and it was pointless to speculate regarding something that could hold such infinite possibilities.

'I am going to bed,' he said.

21

A Lesson

The good time came to an abrupt and sickening end for the gang of three late one evening when Kimberley walked into the house crying her eyes out and with a blood-soaked rag held to her face.

The three had been playing cards at the table in the kitchen, gambling for small stakes because none of them had the necessary cash for anything higher. They heard the front door being opened and shut, and Harker, who was dealing, stopped with a card in one hand and the rest of the pack in the other.

'Sounds like our Kim. Back early. I wonder why.'

They did not have to wait long for the answer. She must have guessed where they would be, and she pushed the door open and walked in. They were so shocked they all stood up, sliding their chairs back and dropping the cards.

'My God, Kim!' Tulley said. 'What happened to you?'

There were bloodstains all down the front

of her dress, though the blood appeared to have stopped dripping. She was in a mess, her hair all tangled, miniskirt torn, bruises on her arms and legs. Somewhere she had lost her shoes and her feet were dirty.

She did not answer the question. She had come to a halt just inside the room and the tears were flowing, though she was making no sound except for a kind of low whimper like an animal in distress. Tulley put a hand on her right arm and guided her to a chair which he had just vacated. She sat down, and she was shivering as if cold, the bloodstained rag still held to her face.

Again he asked: 'What happened? How did you get like this?'

She answered with one word, speaking hardly above a whisper.

'Lammy.'

'He did this to you?'

'Yes.'

'The bastard!'

Starke said: 'What's he done to your face? Why all the blood?'

She took the rag away so that they could see for themselves. The cuts were on each cheek. They formed two crosses, and they had bled a lot at first, though the bleeding had eased now.

'He caught me. I was alone. He dragged

me into a dark alleyway and I couldn't get away. He said I'd been a bad girl running out on him and he had to learn me a lesson so as none of the others got the same ideas into their heads. He said he'd mark me so's I'd never be able to work the streets again. And then he cut me.'

'What'd he use?'

'Razor blade. It hurt. It still hurts. He knocked me about too. The way he does when he's mad at you. Then he let me go.'

'I'll kill him,' Starke said. 'I'll kill the bloody swine.'

'Oh, sure,' Tulley said. 'All in good time. But that ain't going to help her right now. By rights she oughter be in a hospital.'

It was the victim herself who vetoed that idea. It seemed to scare her.

'No, not that. No hospital.'

They could understand her objection. In a hospital she would be asked too many awkward questions. They would want to know who she was; what she was doing in London; how she had come by her injuries. They might inform the police, of whose attentions she appeared to be in great dread.

She was also, for much the same reason, opposed to the suggestion that she might see a doctor. And no one seemed much inclined to press either idea, since they themselves were less than eager to bring the matter to the attention of anyone in authority. It impinged too closely on their own activities, and they were already characters of more than a little interest to the likes of DCI Stephen Cartwright and DS William Brown. They were not sure whether these officers were aware that they had a fourth person sharing their accommodation with them, and they certainly had no wish to draw attention to this state of affairs. Life was complicated enough as it was.

Strictly speaking of course they were breaking the law by living, at least to some extent, on the immoral earnings of a prostitute, but they were in the habit of acting so much in ways that could hardly have been described as legal that one more variety hardly bothered them. And besides, surely the police had too much already on their hands without bothering to bring charges on such petty transgressions as that. This was the way in which Tulley reasoned it; and he was fairly certain that Cartwright would be far more interested in nailing one of the gang for the murder of Chuck Brogan than for anything as unimportant as that of giving shelter to a young hooker.

There was also the matter of a cache of gold bullion, the whereabouts of which they were all deeply interested in, including without doubt one, Stephen Cartwright.

But for the present the most pressing matter was that of attending to Kim's injuries; and if hospitals and doctors were ruled out it had to be up to the three men themselves to do what they could for her. There was no first-aid kit in the house, so Harker was dispatched to find a chemist's shop that was open late and buy Dettol and dressings and Elastoplast.

He went at once, taking the car, and while he was gone the other two helped the girl to get cleaned up as much as possible. A little blood was still oozing from the cuts on her cheeks; the razor blade had sliced fairly deeply and it was evident that when the wounds had healed she would be scarred for life with those two crosses on her face. Lammy Buller had done a thorough job of ruining her looks.

'We'll make him pay for this,' Tulley said. 'He won't get away with it. He just don't know what's going to hit him.'

Starke was in full agreement with that.

'The sod's overreached hisself this time. He shoulda bin sorted out years ago.'

'Too true.'

Thinking of what they might do to Lammy when they caught up with him eased their feelings a little, but not a great deal. He had done too much damage, not only to the girl, but to them also indirectly. With his damned razor blade he had thrown everything out of gear for them. They had had a sweet little arrangement; things jogging along nicely while they waited to get their hands on the big prize, the one they still had in the foreground of their minds. Kim had been supplying the means of keeping them afloat while they waited for Caley to make his move; but now she had become a liability rather than an asset, and it would be up to them to keep her unless they kicked her out. This latter possibility occurred to Tulley, but he rejected it out of hand. He did not believe that any one of them would be prepared to go that far. She was one of them.

★ ★ ★

When Harker came back with the first-aid gear Tulley did what was necessary. She now had her cheeks covered with a dressing of lint and adhesive tape. It stopped the bleeding, but they all knew that when the cuts had healed she would not look the same as before Buller got to work on her.

She cried a lot; not making any sound but

just letting the tears fall, soaking the dressings.

'It'll be all right,' Tulley said. 'Won't take long to heal. You're young. You'll see.'

'There'll be scars, though. I'll look horrible.'

'Scars, yes. But there's surgeons what can do wonders these days with skin grafts and that. They'll make you as good as new.'

'It'll cost though. Where's the money coming from?'

'We'll have the money. Like I told you, we're all going to be as rich as creases.'

She did not believe it. They could see that. She was really depressed and nothing they said was going to cheer her up.

'That Lammy bastard,' Starke muttered. 'He's got it coming to him.'

*   *   *

But not for a while. They had to find him first. And he was proving elusive. Possibly he realised he might have overstepped the mark and left himself exposed to reprisals, which could be severe.

It was no secret in the underworld that Tulley's lot were keen to have a meeting with Lammy Buller, and since nobody liked the pimp, they had plenty of tips regarding his whereabouts. But he was a crafty operator and he was never at the place where he had been reported to be when they got there. It was as if he had a sixth sense which warned him when they were coming, and he would have left before they arrived.

But even the smartest of foxes cannot always elude the hounds. Tulley, Harker and Starke were dedicated to their task and would not abandon the search. So in the end they ran Lammy to earth in a public house called The Stoat and Rabbit in the East End, which was pretty crowded at that hour in the evening.

They failed to spot him at first, but then they caught sight of him standing by the bar at the far end of the room. They worked their way towards him through the crush, and they were pretty close to him before he became aware of their presence. He looked scared then, and if they had not been between him and the exit he might well have tried to beat them to it. But he was hemmed in and there was no way of escape. He could only stand and wait for them to come to him. And maybe he was figuring that they would never attempt any rough stuff with all those people standing around.

When they had edged their way to him Tulley said: 'Well, if it ain't our old friend,

Lammy Buller! How you doin', Lam?'

Buller said nothing. He just looked at them — nervously.

'Lost your tongue hey? Well, what you say to taking a little walk with me and my two pals? It's a nice evening.'

Being polite, Tulley was.

Buller was rather less so. He just said: 'Piss off.'

'Only if you piss off with us,' Tulley said. Still being polite, but with menace in the politeness. 'Come on now, Lammy. A stroll in the open air would do you a power of good. Get this fug out of your lungs.'

'You're harassing me,' Buller said. He appealed to those around him. 'This man is harassing me.'

No one seemed interested. Mind your own business was obviously the motto. Don't get involved in anything that isn't to your own advantage. Possibly some of them knew Lammy by sight and would not have thrown him a lifebuoy if he had been drowning in the Thames.

Starke and Harker had now edged themselves close up to Buller, one on each side. They took a grip on his arms and started forcing him towards the exit, with Tulley giving a little help from behind. The throng opened up in front of them, letting them through in spite of Lammy's appeals for aid.

They came out onto the forecourt where the Renault was parked. Lammy Buller put up a bit of a struggle, but he was overpowered and bundled into the back with Starke and Harker squeezing in also, one on each side of him. Tulley got into the driver's seat and started the engine.

'Where you taking me?' Buller demanded.

'You'll see soon enough,' Starke said.

'You're abducting me. That's against the law. I could have you done for this.'

It made the others laugh: the idea of Lammy appealing to the coppers.

'You shouldn't've done what you did,' Harker said. 'Not to a nice girl like that. Just because she ran away from you. What'd you expect when you treated her like dirt?'

Buller tried to excuse himself. 'I helped her when she came to the Smoke. She didn't have nothing then.'

'Helped yourself, more like. You think you owned her?'

Buller had nothing to say to that. He lapsed into silence and they could tell he was scared. He had good reason to be.

★　★　★

It was not a long journey. The place they eventually came to was a piece of waste ground which had once had a small factory on it. All that remained of the building now was a ruin of fallen tiles, crumbling walls and broken glass. No doubt eventually the site would be cleared and developed, possibly with private houses and even a shopping centre, but for the present it was simply wasteland.

Tulley stopped the car and switched off the ignition.

'This looks a likely spot.'

Hawker and Starke agreed. Buller was becoming more and more scared. He was not at all happy with the way things were going.

'Think we oughter gag him now?' Starke said. 'Don't want him screaming his bloody head off and disturbing the neighbours. Not that it looks like there are any.'

They had come prepared for this. Tulley fished a roll of brown adhesive tape out of the glove compartment and handed it to Starke. Buller put up a rather half-hearted resistance to the gagging procedure, but he seemed to realise it was hopeless and finally gave in. Starke bound two layers of tape over his mouth and round the back of his neck. It was going to be a difficult and painful task to peel it off.

The rest of the operation was brutal, but it did not take long. They hauled Buller out of the car and dragged him round to the back of the derelict building. There they threw him down and broke both of his arms. They kicked him in the chest and probably fractured some ribs too; though of this they could not be certain. Finally Starke and Harker held him down while Tulley took a razor blade from his pocket and carved two bloody crosses on his cheeks.

'Tit-for-tat, Lammy,' he said. 'Tit-for-tat. Now you know what it feels like.'

He felt a degree of satisfaction at having taken revenge for what Buller had done to Kimberley, as did the other two. It did nothing to repair the damage to her cheeks of course; she would be scarred and disfigured for the rest of her life. But Lammy would be too; and the arms and ribs would be painful for a long time.

Maybe it would teach him a lesson. Maybe in future he would treat his girls rather better and even cut down on the lamming.

But this was doubtful.

22

A Call on Caley

The belief held by Tulley, Starke and Harker that the police were unaware of the presence in their house of the girl named Kimberley was not as well founded as they imagined. The forces of law and order knew quite a bit about her, but they were taking no action for the present because Detective Chief Inspector Cartwright was holding them in check. And besides, they had so much work on their hands and were so lacking in resources that only the more pressing matters could be attended to.

Cartwright kept his ear to the ground, or rather he kept junior officers' ears to the ground and picked up information from them. Thus he heard rumours of the affair that had led to the injuries sustained by Lammy Buller, but he took no action.

Buller had broken arms and ribs that required hospital treatment, but he insisted that these had been caused by a fall from a ladder. No one believed this, since he had never been known to do anything as energetic as climbing a ladder, and it hardly explained how the cuts on his cheeks came to be there. But since he steadfastly refused to accuse anyone of attacking him and stuck to his story, nothing more could be done about it. Moreover, the general opinion was that he had had it coming to him for a long time and had simply got what he deserved.

Cartwright himself had a good reason for taking the softly, softly approach to the gang of three. He still believed that they or Alan Caley might eventually lead him to the discovery of the gold that he was convinced Chuck Brogan had hidden before being arrested and sent to jail.

This gold had become something of an obsession with Cartwright. Which probably had to do with the fact that he had worked on the case in his younger days and felt that he had been outwitted by a cunning rogue. Now there were other rogues trying to outwit him, and he was determined to see that they did not.

As he remarked to Detective Sergeant Brown: 'We're as close to getting to the root of that business as we've ever been. I'm damn sure of it.'

Brown himself was not quite so sure, but he did not say so. 'You still think Brogan gave Caley some information?'

'I feel certain he did. And that other lot think so too; you can bet your life on that. They'll have been keeping a sharp eye on him to see what moves he makes. He'll know that of course, and he'll be mighty careful.'

'Well, if Brogan did tip Caley off to the place where he hid the stuff, the man must think he's in luck. Now he'll cop the lot all for himself.'

'If he can get away with it. Which may not be easy. Where do you go to find a buyer for half a ton of gold bars?'

'Was there half a ton?'

'I don't know. The exact amount was never revealed. But even half that would still be a nice little haul.'

'True. And easier to handle.'

Cartwright sucked his teeth. 'It's hardly the kind of packet your common or garden fence is going to welcome with open arms, is it? Gold watches, yes. Gold earrings, yes again. But even one bar of the raw stuff? I doubt it.'

Besides having a long, bony frame and a stoop, Cartwright had a bald head which had a somewhat yellowy tinge and a few bumps here and there. Now he smoothed down a few surviving hairs which he seemed to cherish long after they had ceased to serve any useful purpose, protective or decorative, and let his gaze rest on the sergeant.

'Got any suggestions, Bill?'

Detective Sergeant Brown gave some thought to the matter but failed to come up with any constructive contribution.

'Don't see what more we can do.'

He himself had no irresistible urge to locate the cache of gold. He had not been involved in the original investigation and did not feel the kind of resentment that Cartwright did at being outwitted by a crook like Chuck Brogan. Now it seemed that he was being foiled once again, and he did not like it.

'I think,' he said, 'it might be a good idea if you went to pay friend Caley a visit.'

Brown did not think it was much of an idea, but he did not say so.

'Get him talking,' Cartwright said. 'He may let something slip without thinking. Nose around a bit. You know the drill.'

'I'll do my best. But of course we still don't know for certain that Brogan told him anything.'

'Oh, he did, he did.'

It was something Cartwright refused not to believe. So much depended on it.

★ ★ ★

Detective Sergeant William Brown drove his car into Caley's yard with some reluctance.

He did not anticipate that any good would come of the visit, but he had to go through the motions to please his superior officer.

Caley was in his office, doing nothing much except brooding on the wretched manner in which things had turned out for him. He heard the car come to a halt, and went to the window and saw Brown getting out of it. He recognised the detective sergeant at once, having seen him and even spoken to him on previous occasions.

His first reaction was one of alarm; it was the way he responded to the sight of any policeman ever since that ill-fated luncheon date with Chuck Brogan. He could never rid himself of a feeling of guilt, even though he had done nothing more reprehensible than concealing the fact that Brogan had given him a small envelope with a cryptic sketch map inside it before being snuffed out by a petty criminal with a gun.

And what benefit had he gained from it? None at all. It would have been different if there had now been a load of gold bullion secreted in one of his sheds. But there was not; and there never would have been even if things had gone strictly according to plan. Because he would not have brought it to London; he would have scuttled off with the stuff to some other part of the country and would never have shown his face in the metropolis again.

Sweet dreams, now faded for ever.

★ ★ ★

He heard Brown give a rat-a-tat-tat with the knocker and thought for a moment of pretending he was not at home. Second thoughts told him that the sergeant had probably glimpsed him at the window and would not be fooled. And after all, what had he to fear? His hands were clean. Or nearly so.

He went to the door and opened it, and Brown said: 'Good afternoon, Mr Caley. May I come in?'

For a moment Caley had an impulse to say: 'No, you may not.' But then he decided that this might be unwise. It was best not to antagonise a police officer. And besides, might it not be regarded as an admission of a guilty conscience?

So he said, rather grudgingly: 'I suppose so.'

Brown came in and Caley closed the door and led him into the sitting room, which seemed to be accommodating a wide variety of visitors lately: police officers, crooks and Martine; all, in one way or another, looking, as it were, for the pot of gold at the foot of the rainbow.

Brown sat down and cast a glance round the room.

'Nice place you have here.'

Caley was quite sure the sergeant did not really think it was a nice place. Like the rest of the property, the room was in a seedy, run-down condition, and they both knew it.

'You didn't come here to tell me that.'

'True enough.'

'I suppose it's about that gold.'

'That's so. We'd still like to find out where Brogan hid it.'

'If he ever had it.'

'Oh, he had it all right. You can be sure of that.'

Caley took out a cigarette and lit it, but did not offer one to Brown. He assumed the police officer was a non-smoker, at least when he was on duty. And besides, cigarettes cost money, and there was not very much of that swilling around in Caley's vicinity just then.

'Well,' he said, 'I don't see how I can help you. I've told your lot all I know already.'

'You're sure of that? You haven't remembered something Brogan may have said to you which would give us a clue?'

'No. Nothing.'

'And he didn't even mention the bullion robbery?'

'Not a word.'

He could say this with perfect confidence because it, unlike some of the answers he had given, was the solid truth. Brogan had never once touched on the subject.

Detective Sergeant Brown had had enough experience of interrogating people to have a shrewd idea when they were holding something back. He had the impression that Caley was doing this now. And yet he rather doubted whether Brogan had in fact put so much confidence in his old acquaintance as to tell him straight out where the gold was hidden. Surely the two men had not been sufficiently close for him to put that much trust in an old school pal whom he was meeting for the first time in years. It just did not make sense.

And yet he must have had something to impart; otherwise, why the meeting, the luncheon date, immediately he came out of prison? Now that really was the question.

Before leaving Brown suggested that Caley might show him round the premises.

'You think I may have a pile of gold lying around somewhere?' Caley said.

He gave a nervous laugh, and wished he had not, because the look that Brown gave him suggested that this was no laughing matter.

'You haven't, have you?'

'Of course not. Just kidding. Let's go.'

★　★　★

The tour of inspection revealed to the sergeant just how run-down the place was. House and outhouses were in dire need of painting and a good deal of repair; and of course almost all of the building material had been sold off to postpone the evil hour when the cash would run out.

There was, however, one implement that seemed to stand out simply by reason of its gleaming newness — a spade that looked as if it had never been used.

'You a gardener, Mr Caley?'

The question took Caley off guard, and he answered quickly: 'Gardener! Lord, no! Do you see any garden in this place? Why do you ask?'

'The spade. Looks brand new.'

'Oh that,' Caley said. And he was cursing himself for leaving it lying around when he had taken it off the pick-up truck. He groped in his brain for a good story to explain the presence of the implement and all he could come up with was something about a man who ordered it and then had never come to pick it up. 'Left it on my hands.'

Which hardly explained why it had not gone with the other stuff that had been sold off at knock-down prices.

He was relieved when Brown did not pursue the matter. He had no further questions and very soon took his leave.

★ ★ ★

Detective Sergeant Brown returned to the station and reported to his superior the outcome of his visit.

'He knows something, sir, but he's holding it back. I'd make a bet on that. He's got a guilty conscience, and it shows. He's an amateur, you see, not your ordinary, run-of-the-mill villain who'll lie his head off without batting an eyelid. It doesn't come natural to him, if you see what I mean.'

Cartwright did see. After all, he had had even more experience of the world of crooks than Brown had.

'And then,' Brown said, bringing out his clincher, 'there's the spade.'

'Spade?'

'Brand new. All other tools gone, but this new spade is there. Cock-and-bull story that he got it for a customer who never came to pick it up. Very thin, that.'

'And you think this spade may have been intended to be used for digging up some gold bars?'

'I'd say it was a possibility.'

'But it hasn't been used?'

'Not yet.'

Cartwright did some more sucking of teeth. Then: 'Seems to me we'd better keep an eye even more closely on our good friend, Mr Caley. Don't you think so?'

'It might be a good idea,' Brown admitted.

23

Collection

It was a little after one o'clock in the morning when Oliver Danby brought his Range Rover to a halt at the side of a very minor road. The place he had chosen was less than half a mile from the edge of the high cliffs beyond which lay the broad expanse of the English Channel. Between the road and the cliff edge was a stretch of open ground across which a narrow footpath had been trodden out in the course of time by a succession of holidaymakers and others.

Some distance away to the east was a caravan park with only a few lights visible at this time of night. No sound could be heard from that direction. Indeed, all was quiet as Danby got out of the car.

He was dressed all in black — shoes, trousers, shirt, wind-cheater and baseball cap. He had also lightly blacked his face and was wearing black leather gloves. There was no moon, but the sky was practically free of cloud cover and the stars shed a silvery radiance which enabled Danby to find his way along the footpath without making him visible at more than a few yards from the track.

This rough pathway came to an end at the edge of the cliff, and here a narrow V-shaped gully sloped fairly steeply down to the beach some way below. Even in daylight it would have been a descent that only an active and reasonably athletic person with no fear of heights would have attempted. It was not, however, quite as difficult as it looked, since rough steps had been hacked into it in the steepest places.

In darkness it was inevitably more hazardous, but Danby had no qualms. He had made the descent by night and subsequent climb back up on a number of previous occasions and he regarded this part of his nocturnal journey with no more trepidation than the journey from London, where he was staying for a day or two at a modest hotel.

His eyes had become accustomed to the darkness by the time he reached the cliff edge, and he had no difficulty in making out the top of the gully. Facing inward and aiding his descent with both hands, he quickly made his way to the beach.

The Channel was as calm as it had been when he had anchored *Osprey* offshore and made his visit to the cave. Now he had to walk no more than fifty yards or so in order to reach it again. Inside it was completely dark, but he had no trouble in finding the spot where he had buried the kitbag.

He began digging immediately with the small shovel he had carried inside his windcheater. Very soon he had lifted out the kitbag and was filling in the hole with the loose sand. He had scarcely completed this task and was about to leave the cave when he heard voices outside and froze.

His immediate fear was that somehow customs officers or the police had decided to search the beach, having by some means or other had their suspicions aroused that a smuggling operation might be taking place along that strip of coastline.

He dismissed this idea almost immediately when it became apparent that there were only two voices, a man's and a woman's, or possibly a girl's.

It was a nuisance nevertheless. Certainly it was a remarkably warm night, but at that hour one would hardly have expected anyone to be taking a stroll along the beach. The girl seemed to be giggling rather a lot and he hazarded a guess that both of them had been drinking before deciding to go for a walk. Possibly they had broken away from a late night party so that they could be on their own.

They drew level with the entrance to the cave and came to a halt. Danby could just make out their shadowy forms, and the thought struck him that they might decide to enter the cave; which would be the devil. But they showed no inclination to do that, and he saw no reason why they should.

Then he heard the man say: 'How about a dip in the briny?'

'Oh, yes, let's,' the girl said. 'It'll be fun.'

Danby could discern their movements as they began to shed what few clothes they had on; and the girl was doing some more of the rather tipsy giggling. A moment later they were moving out of his line of sight, leaving a little pile of clothing near the entrance to the cave.

He debated with himself whether to leave at once before they came back or wait until they left the scene altogether; and he was still hesitating when he heard them returning and knew that he had lost the opportunity.

He heard the girl say: 'I didn't think the water would have been so cold.' And he guessed that they had taken the briefest of dips and then had retreated.

They were back now at the spot where they had left their clothes and he could imagine them shivering.

'We should have brought a towel,' the girl said. Her teeth were chattering and she was no doubt regretting the wild impulse that had led to the chilly immersion.

The man laughed. 'I'll give you a rub down. That'll warm you up in no time.'

After which it was apparent from the sound of things that he was doing exactly as he had proposed. The girl was giving little squeals and doing some more of the giggling. Danby could just detect the movements of the two naked bodies and he felt like a voyeur, especially when they slipped to the ground and apparently got down to some more serious business.

It was the devil. As long as they were there they had him trapped in the cave and time was getting away. He was impatient to be back in the car and on his way, but he had to curb that impatience while this shadowy couple, whose faces he could not see, enjoyed themselves not ten yards away from him. He just hoped they did not decide to spend the rest of the night there.

They did not do that, but by the time they finally moved away he had lost more than an hour. It was not disastrous but it was annoying. He was a man who liked things to proceed strictly according to plan. His plan. Now it would be even later than usual when he got back to the hotel in London which he regularly used when carrying out this part of the operation.

He heard the man and the girl talking and laughing as they walked away, and he gave them time to get clear before emerging from the darkness of the cave with the kitbag on his shoulder. He scaled the cliff without difficulty by way of the gully, and shortly after that was at the roadway where the Range Rover was parked.

With the kitbag stowed away in the boot and the blacking wiped from his face with a cloth, he started the vehicle, turned it and drove away. The delay caused by the amorous couple still irked him slightly, but it was really a small matter and had not seriously disrupted the smooth execution of his business. Five minutes later he had come to a crossroads, had taken the turning to the right and was heading for London.

⋆   ⋆   ⋆

Day was breaking when he reached his destination, the hotel which he had left the previous day. He parked the Range Rover, took the kitbag from the boot and checked in. A sleepy night porter handed him the key to his room and gave him a curious look but asked no questions. If a guest chose to stay out all night and arrive early in the morning carrying a large canvas bag, it was none of his business. You got all sorts in a hotel of that kind. Best not to enquire too closely into the activities of some of them.

Danby went to his room, locked the door after having hung a notice on the outside that he was not to be disturbed, undressed and got into bed. It was a long time since he had had any sleep, and now he slept soundly even though he was using the kitbag as a pillow.

As a precaution.

24

Financial Transaction

The meal that Danby had when he awoke might have been a very late breakfast or an early lunch. It was makeshift and grudgingly provided in his room, but he was not bothered. Food was not his chief concern at that time.

Later he called a number on his mobile phone. It was a man's voice that answered with one word: 'Yes?' Hoarse, not entirely friendly.

Danby replied with one word also: 'Clayhanger.'

The hoarse voice completed the exchange with yet another single word: 'Excalibur.' But this time there was rather more warmth in it.

The exchange of words had been brief and cryptic, but it satisfied Danby. He took a large empty suitcase from the wardrobe and began to transfer the packets of cocaine from the kitbag to this. When he had done so he closed and locked the suitcase, carried it down to the Range Rover, put it in the boot and drove away.

His destination, reached in some three-quarters of an hour, was a house of no architectural distinction whatever, situated in a tree-lined residential street with rows of similar houses on each side; all with bay windows and tiny, somewhat neglected front gardens.

Danby parked the Range Rover outside one of these dwellings and took the suitcase from the boot. There were steps leading up to the front door. Possibly in days gone by they had been kept white by an overworked housemaid, commonly known as a skivvy; but now they were a dirty grey in colour and cracked in places. The house was such a one as Mr Pooter might have lived in. It was at the end of the row and had a side door at which tradesmen would have called.

Danby was not a tradesman, except of a rather unusual kind, and he did not go to the side door. Instead, he ascended the steps that had once been white, put his thumb on a button that was of much later date than the house and heard the faint sound of a bell ringing somewhere within.

After a minute or so a man came to open the door. He was black and he was a giant; maybe some twenty stone of bone and muscle. He had a shaven head and there were old scars above his eyes which indicated that he had probably been a professional boxer, but not one skilful enough to avoid a deal of punishment in the ring. As a doorkeeper he was the kind who might have intimidated anyone of a nervous disposition, but Danby was not intimidated. He had seen the man on several previous occasions; so he just said:

'Okay, Pete. Let's go. I'm expected.'

'Sure,' the black said. 'Walk right in.'

He stood aside to let Danby pass, then closed the door and locked it. They were now in a tiled hallway, with carpetless stairs leading up from it.

The man called Pete led the way up the stairs, Danby following with the suitcase. There was an odd, rather unpleasant smell about the house. It could have been the odour of decay. It had seen better days.

The room they went to was on the first floor. It was fairly large and might once have been the main bedroom. There was no bed in it now and not much other furniture: no dressing-table, no wardrobe, no chest of drawers. There were a couple of wooden chairs, a safe, a kitchen table with a spring balance standing on it, a washbasin attached to one wall, a cracked mirror behind it which had maybe brought somebody seven years of bad luck, cigarette butts and a lot of other rubbish on a bare wooden floor, much worm-eaten in places and smelling of dry rot.

There had been just one man in the room until Danby and Pete entered. He was, in sharp contrast to the black, a stunted individual, little taller than a dwarf. As if to make up for the lack of height, he was fat, a true roly-poly of a man, bulging in all directions. He was affable too, welcoming Danby in with a smile and a cordial greeting. It was hard to associate him with the gruff, somewhat unfriendly voice that had answered the telephone when Danby rang. Perhaps he had two personas, either of which he could present as the situation demanded.

'Nice to see you again, Mr X. You been keeping well?'

'Reasonably so.'

He would have made a bet that the roly-poly man didn't give a damn about the state of his health except in so far as it impinged on the business that was from time to time transacted between the two of them. The name he used in his dealing with Danby was Robinson, but Danby felt pretty certain that this was not his real name. In this kind of business people tended to be wary of revealing their true identity or anything else about themselves. Thus Danby himself was always referred to and addressed as Mr X, though he could never be certain that the man who called himself Robinson did not know more about him than he had ever admitted.

Still, however much he did or did not know, he was hardly likely to go running to the police with information that could lead to the termination of a business arrangement that was so highly profitable to both of them. That there might be other, shadowy figures somewhere in the background who pulled Mr Robinson's strings was of course a possibility, but if there were, Danby had never come into contact with them; and he did not wish to do so. They would probably be the kind who would hardly think twice about snuffing you out if it suited their purpose to do so.

Pete had sat down on one of the hard chairs which creaked under his weight but stood the strain. He lit a cigarette and dropped the dead match on the floor to join the other garbage.

Danby put the suitcase on the table, unlocked it and raised the lid to reveal the bags of cocaine.

'Nice,' Robinson said. 'Very nice.'

He took one of the bags out of the case, laid it on the table and made a slit in it with a penknife. He fetched a cup of water from the cold tap over the washbowl and scooped up a little of the cocaine with a spatula. He tipped this into the water and watched it dissolve completely. Danby knew that if the drug had been laced with sugar it would not have done so.

'Okay?' he said.

'So far.'

But there was another test with some chemical, the name of which Danby could never remember. Something to do with cobalt, he believed. You mixed it in with some of the coke, and if it came up with a deep blue colour as it dissolved you knew you had the pure product, high-class cocaine. If the colour was paler you knew the drug had been laced. It was not the genuine high-grade article.

Danby's sample passed both tests.

'Don't you trust me yet?' he asked.

Robinson gave a smile. 'In this business trust is something best left out.'

'Have you ever known me bring you low grade product?'

'There's always a first time. Tell me, do you ever see it tested when you pick it up at the other end?'

Danby had to admit that he did not.

'So you see — '

'But what would they gain by cheating? It

could kill the trade.'

'Maybe so. But I like to be on the safe side anyway.'

He weighed the bags — each of them. Then he went to an old safe that was standing against one wall, unlocked it and took out some bundles of banknotes in British currency. He handed these to Danby who riffled through them before stowing them in the suitcase. Mr Robinson watched him with some amusement. 'You're not going to count them?'

'No. It's the same argument. What would you stand to gain by cheating me? You'd lose a supplier. How much is there here?'

'Four hundred K. It's a lot of money.'

'Not nearly as much as your lot will get when it goes on the streets. But it won't be the same stuff, will it?'

This was the truth. It would have been converted into crack and the value would have gone sky high. Crack was the new disease, the new plague. It got its hooks into the users, kids very often, and they could not break free. It had been almost a gentlemanly thing to snort coke; it might eat your nose away, but it took time. Crack took no time at all and there was nothing classy about it.

But he was not involved in that part of the business. His was the clean part, the ocean voyage, the smuggling of the basic commodity ashore, the bulk selling to the middleman who would modify it and pass it on to the pushers, who were often addicts themselves.

Danby had managed to convince himself that his hands were clean — or almost so. Therefore, it was with a clear conscience that he locked the suitcase, carried it down the stairs and allowed Pete to open the front door for him.

He stowed a small fortune in the boot of the Range Rover and drove away.

★   ★   ★

He decided not to spend another night in London. He returned to the hotel, paid the bill and collected his luggage. It was about half-past three in the afternoon when he set out on the journey back to Norfolk, and he went first to the office in Norwich.

Angela Crowe had already left when he arrived at the building, but he let himself into the office and locked the door behind him. It was most improbable that anyone would have walked in even if he had left the door unlocked, but there was no point in taking any unnecessary risk. He did not wish to be disturbed while he was stowing away four hundred thousand pounds sterling in a safe that was far more modern and thief-proof than the one from which the man who called himself Robinson had taken it in London.

Having thus disposed of the cash for the present, he took one glance round the office, which still retained a hint of Miss Crowe's perfume, and departed.

Half an hour later he was at his own house.

25

To Fresh Woods

The fact that Cynthia's Mercedes was not in the garage or parked outside told him that she was not at home. It did not surprise him, and it did not bother him either. Her movements were of very little interest to him these days; as little indeed as he imagined his were to her. They had really drifted apart since those early passionate days of their marriage and were never likely to come together again. Well, it was the kind of thing that happened. To his way of thinking, it was inevitable.

He let himself into the house and went first to the kitchen with the intention of making himself a meal of some kind. He had had nothing to eat since that late breakfast at the hotel, and he was feeling ravenous.

And that was when he saw the note.

It was propped up with a cup on the table where they had been in the habit of taking their meals when there was no need for ceremony. It was a single sheet of paper folded once, so that only the inscription,

Oliver, was visible.

Somehow he had a presentiment of what he would find when he unfolded the paper, so he was not surprised even by the laconic nature of the message. Nevertheless, he felt a touch of pique. For this was something he had had in mind himself. Confound it, he had even mentioned it to her. And now she had taken it upon herself to decide without even the formality of a final conference with him. It was just not good enough.

The note was certainly brief. And yet he supposed it said all that was necessary to say.

'This is by way of goodbye. I doubt whether you will be devastated by my departure. After all, it had to come, didn't it? C.'

He gave a laugh. Of course it had to come. Did she really believe he had been blissfully ignorant of her latest affair with that fellow Dryden? The man was a multi-millionaire and Danby himself had never been in the same league. When Dryden's yacht was mentioned one was not referring to a little cockleshell like *Osprey* but to a floating palace which accommodated large parties of guests and could often be found hanging around the Mediterranean playgrounds of the stinking rich. In contemplating life on board such a vessel Cynthia's dislike of the sea would have been thrust into the background. Dryden had beckoned and she had responded. What else could have been expected of her?

Danby tore the note into little pieces and scattered them on the floor. After which he set about preparing the meal which he was so greatly in need of. While he did so and again while he ate he devoted some thought to the situation as it had now developed.

The fact was that matters had been simplified. He could see his future moves more clearly. He would of course sell the house. He had never cared much for it. It had been more Cynthia's choice than his at a time when he had still been infatuated enough to let her have her way in most things. Now he had only himself to please.

He went to bed early and was asleep almost immediately.

★ ★ ★

The news had probably been on television and radio the previous evening, but Danby had missed both and was not aware of an event that affected him more than a little until he read about it in the morning paper.

It gave him a shock, even though it was not until he had read the report a second time that he realised just how narrow an escape he had had. Then it really began to sink in. He had been within a whisker of meeting an untimely death.

From the report he gathered that two men had been shot in a house in a rather seedy residential area of south London. There was a picture of the house, which he recognised at once, since he had visited it the previous day. A witness said that he was walking down the street and saw a car parked outside the house, which was at the end of a row. He then heard a number of what sounded like gunshots coming from the house. He halted about twenty yards from the car, and a few minutes later he saw two men come out of the house in a great hurry. One of them was carrying a large bag, which he threw into the back of the car. Then both men got in and drove away at high speed.

The witness also stated that both men were black.

* * *

He called the police on his mobile phone and they arrived very shortly. They discovered two men, dead from gunshot wounds in an upper room. One was black, the other white. Neither had yet been identified, but the police were treating the incident as a gangland killing, possibly connected with drug trafficking. They were appealing to anyone who might be able to provide information regarding the shooting to come forward.

Danby could have given some very useful information if he had wished to do so, but there was no way he was going to step forward. He reckoned that the killers must have arrived quite soon after his departure. If they had been a little earlier they would have had an even bigger haul — not only the cocaine but also the money he had been paid for it. And then there would have been three dead bodies lying on the floor of that filthy room.

The police were almost certainly right in believing that it was a gangland killing. He guessed that the two blacks who had pumped bullets into Mr Robinson and Pete were probably Jamaican Yardies, gangsters with their fingers in the illicit drug racket. There was a lot of rivalry in such a lucrative trade, and it could be fatal for some.

Well, one thing was certain now: he was out of it. This incident clinched it for him. Even if he had wished to continue bringing the stuff in, how would he have disposed of it? His connection was gone, and he did not fancy the job of trying to find another. Not when it seemed to have become such a lethal occupation.

Fortunately, he still had money. Admittedly, he was not a multi-millionaire, but he was not short of a bob or two. Perhaps the time had come to close down the bogus export-import business and branch out in some other activity. He was not yet sure just what; but he would think of something. Life had not ended for him as it had for those two unfortunates in that dingy old house in London.

Was it not Milton who wrote: 'Tomorrow to fresh woods and pastures new.'?

It was really not such a bad idea.

26

With Violence

It was fast approaching crisis time for the gang of three. The cuts on Kimberley's cheeks were healing; but there were scabs on them, and later there would be unsightly scars. For the present she was doing very little but mope around the house. All the spirit seemed to have gone out of her, and she was of course bringing in no money.

No one else was feeding the kitty either. The three men had come to rely on the girl for day to day expenses while they waited for Caley to lead them to the pot of gold. It was pie in the sky, but none of them was willing to face the fact. They had waited so long for the fortune to drop into their hands that they could not bring themselves to doubt that it ever would.

Now, however, with the ready money fast dribbling away, it became absolutely imperative that action of some sort should be taken.

'We'll have to do a job,' Tulley said. 'There's no two ways about it. We can't live on air.'

They all knew what a job in that context signified. It was just a way of saying that they had to make a transfer of cash from someone else's pocket to theirs. In other words, carry out a robbery.

It was quite some time since they had last done anything of that description. Indeed, they had been virtually inactive since the shooting of Chuck Brogan in the Top Notch restaurant; a fact that had not gone unnoticed by Detective Chief Inspector Stephen Cartwright.

'They're lying low,' he remarked to Detective Sergeant Brown. 'Just waiting for that fellow Caley to come up with the goods, I shouldn't wonder.'

'Well, he's taking a long time about it,' Brown said. 'I begin to wonder if we aren't barking up the wrong tree. You'd think he'd have made a move by now. With his business down the drain, he must be nearly as pushed for cash as those three villains.'

'Something's got to break soon,' Cartwright said. 'You can be sure of that.'

He was right on this point, though he could not have foreseen what it might be. And yet it was on his patch when it did.

★ ★ ★

The gang had done some reconnoitring in the Renault, leaving Kimberley in the house. They were looking for a soft target, and there were quite a number of them around in the area where they were living. Of course they did not give such a high yield as a bank; but banks tended to be more difficult to rob than a corner shop or a tobacconist's. Their security arrangements were more sophisticated and were enough to discourage such crude operators as Tulley and his lot.

Moreover, the three of them had rather lost confidence since the Top Notch affair. Perhaps it was because they knew the coppers were keeping an eye on them. They guessed that Cartwright was after their blood and that they needed to step warily if they were to avoid his unwanted attentions.

It was something of a surprise to them that there had been no repercussions from the beating-up of Lammy Buller. They could not believe that the Bill had not got to hear of it and knew perfectly well who had carried out the attack. Yet there had been nothing to indicate that they felt the slightest interest in it.

'Can't be bothered, I reckon,' Harker said. 'Meanter say, it ain't as if Lammy was an upright, law-abiding citizen what they need to protect from blokes like us. He's dirt. So why would they waste their time on him? You can bet your life he ain't lodged a complaint.'

In preparation for a resumption of business they had acquired two snub-nosed revolvers in place of the one that had killed Chuck Brogan and had been jettisoned in double quick time. It was easy to pick up shooters at rock-bottom prices these days. Since possession had been made illegal there seemed to be more of them around than there had been before. They were flooding into the country like the duty-free fags and the narcotics; not to mention all the illegal immigrants. The UK seemed to be just one big open market for the smart boys to exploit.

'Sometimes,' Tulley remarked, 'it seems to me like we're in the wrong bloody business. Drugs; that's where the big money is.'

'Maybe so,' Starke said. 'But you try pushing your snout in there and you're likely to be for the chop. It's a lucrative racket, and them what's in it don't take kindly to outsiders trying to muscle in on their territory.'

'Still and all it'd be nice to have the money.'

'We'll be in the money when we get our paws on that gold.'

'Ah, but when'll that be?'

'When Caley makes his move. That's when.'

'Well, I just wish he'd get up off his arse and do it.'

It was what they all wished. It was their future; the glittering dream that had possessed their minds for so long.

★ ★ ★

They chose a small general store owned by a Pakistani who had come to the UK to make his fortune by working all hours. His name, not surprisingly, was Patel. Both he and his wife were well past middle age now. They had raised a family, but the young ones had grown up and gone their own ways, leaving the parents once more to themselves. One of them was a university lecturer and they were all doing very well in their chosen professions. The old Patels had decided that they would keep the shop open for one more year and then retire. They could easily afford to do so, and there was no point in slaving away all your life. Besides, business was not as good as it had been; there were too many supermarkets taking trade away, and now people used Patel's shop at odd times simply as a convenience.

The three crooks had observed the shop on

two or three occasions, parking the Renault a little way down the street. So they knew at about what time Patel usually closed. It was late in the evening, though not as late as it had been in days long past when every penny needed to be gathered in. Nowadays the shop door was usually locked by nine o'clock, the blinds down and the light switched off.

On the evening when the gang had decided to make their raid it was raining slightly, and any pedestrians who happened to be around were hurrying along under umbrellas or hooded anoraks. The Renault came to its parking place some fifty yards from Patel's shop on the opposite side of the road, with Starke at the wheel. The time was then half-past eight and it was already dark, so that the light in the shop showed up brightly and it was possible to see two or three customers inside with Mr Patel serving them. There were only two other shops nearby, and they were both closed. The nearest streetlamp was some distance away, its sickly light blurred by the falling rain.

'You want my opinion,' Starke said, 'we should never have let them Pakis and all the other Wogs into the country. Taking jobs from our guys. Had my way, I'd kick 'em all out; send 'em back where they came from in the first place.'

'Then who would there be for us to rob?' Harker said. And laughed.

By a quarter to nine the last of the customers had left the shop and the pavements were almost deserted. They could see Patel beginning to shut up for the night. He was pulling one of the blinds down.

'Let's go,' Tulley said.

He and Harker pulled on stocking masks, stepped out of the car and ran the short distance across the road and along the pavement to Patel's shop. They were in luck; there was no one around at that moment and they had an unobstructed run to the shop entrance. Traffic on the road was thin, and a solitary car had just gone past. Patel had by then lowered both window blinds and was at the door, reversing the sign to show CLOSED instead of OPEN. He had not yet locked or bolted the door, and the two robbers pushed it open, almost knocking the shopkeeper off his feet.

He uttered a cry of shock and protest, but they were inside now and had the revolvers out so that he could be in no doubt that this was a hold-up. Tulley closed the door, bolted it and lowered the blind. He was fond of a bit of privacy when employed on a job like this.

Meanwhile, Harker was manhandling Mr Patel and getting him to go behind the counter where the cash-register was situated. He had one hand on the man's shoulder and with the other he was ramming the muzzle of the revolver into the small of his back. And so that the victim should make no mistake concerning the situation he was giving him a harsh warning.

'This is a gun, see? And it's loaded. So no tricks, grandad, 'les you want a bullet in the spine.'

Patel was stuttering. 'What you want? Please. What you want?'

Harker sneered: 'Wotcher think? The cash, old man. The takings. Let's 'ave 'em. Pronto.'

'No, no.'

Tulley had finished with the shop door now and was at the front of the counter. He pointed his revolver at Mr Patel.

'Now don't be stupid. Just hand it over and we'll be gone. No harm done. What's a bit of ready cash to you? Bet you got plenty in the bank.'

The shopkeeper appeared to be swayed by this argument. He went to the till and opened it. Business might not have been as brisk as it had been in former days, but there was a considerable quantity of currency notes and coins in the drawer. Harker grabbed a handful of the paper money and stuffed it in his pocket; and this seemed to madden the legitimate owner. It was certainly a crazy thing he did then.

There was a large pair of scissors lying on the counter with blades a good six inches long. Patel grabbed them by the handles and made a lunge at Harker. More by chance than good aiming the point of the scissors struck Harker on the left side just under the lowest rib. Anger at being robbed must have lent power to the elderly man's arm, for the scissor blades penetrated clothing and skin to dig deeply into the soft flesh.

Harker gave a scream of pain and in a kind of reflex action pressed the trigger of the revolver and shot his assailant in the chest. It was probable that the bullet penetrated his heart, for he uttered no sound but simply collapsed on the floor and did not move again.

Tulley was appalled. 'Christ, Slim! You done it now. What you wanter go and shoot the bugger for?'

Patel had still had a grip on the scissors when Harker shot him, and in falling he had pulled them out of the gangster's side. It was his last involuntary action. Harker was moaning. Blood was flowing out of him; he was in pain and he was scared.

'See what he done to me. I'm hurt. I'm hurt bad.'

'Well, we better get you outa here quick. That shot may have been heard. You got the cash?'

Harker had in fact dropped the wad of notes on the floor, and he was in too much pain to bend down and pick them up. Tulley had to move round to the back of the counter to do the job himself.

'Jesus Christ!' he said. 'There's blood on them.'

Nevertheless, he stuffed them into a haversack he had brought for the purpose and added what was left in the till, pushing the shopkeeper's body aside with his foot so that he could get at it.

'Now let's go.'

Harker was leaning on the counter and still groaning. It was impossible to see whether he was looking sick or not because of the stocking pulled over his head; but it was a safe bet that he was.

'You gotta help me, Josh.'

Tulley slung the haversack over one shoulder and put an arm round Harker and hauled him away from the counter. Harker had dropped his gun and he put a hand to his side where the scissors had gone in. He could feel the warm blood oozing out and it had soaked the cloth. It was slippery and there seemed to be so much of it. He wondered whether he was bleeding to death, and the thought frightened him.

With Tulley's help he had reached the opening in the counter and they were heading for the door when a curtain at the back of the shop was pulled aside and a woman appeared. She seemed to be about the same age as Mr Patel and she was wearing a head scarf, so it was pretty easy to guess that she was his wife. She had probably heard the gunshot and had come to see what was going on.

She took one look at Patel's motionless body and the blood and started screaming her head off.

Tulley put a stop to that in a brutal but effective way. He took his supporting arm away from Harker and stepped up to the woman and hit her on the jaw with his revolver. The screaming was cut off in mid-stream and she just slumped to the floor and lay still.

'Now let's get outa here.' Tulley said. And there was a note of urgency in his voice.

Again he had to help Harker, but they got themselves out of the shop and onto the pavement. There was a man with an umbrella approaching, but Tulley pointed the revolver at him and he just turned and ran.

Harker was pretty well a dead weight for

him now, and he had to drag him across the road to where the Renault was waiting. They were nearly run down by a passing car, and the driver hooted furiously to express his anger, but he did not stop. He probably thought they were a couple of drunks.

They got to the Renault, and Starke already had the rear door open and the engine running. He must have heard the gunshot and guessed that something had gone badly wrong. This was confirmed when Tulley and Harker appeared, the one supporting the other. But he asked no questions straightaway; he just got the car moving as soon as they were in the back.

In fact no one uttered a word until they had reached the end of that stretch of road and turned a corner, though Harker was still groaning and shedding his blood on the upholstery.

Then Starke said, really snarling with rage: 'So let's have it. What happened?'

'It was a cock-up,' Tulley said. 'Every goddamn thing went wrong. Slim got hisself stabbed with a pair of scissors and he shot the shopkeeper. The guy's probably dead,'

'Oh fine! Him again! What is it with you, Slim? You trigger happy or something?'

Harker defended himself while gasping with pain. 'Don't blame me. What'd you've done if somebody stuck a bloody great pair of scissors in your side? Self-defence, that's what it was.'

'Self-defence, my arse! He'd already done his worst, hadn't he? He wasn't going to kill you.'

'I ain't so sure about that. I'm bleeding like a stuck pig and I feel real bad.'

'Making a right mess of the seat too. We're never going to get it clean. Suppose the coppers come sniffing around. You think they won't notice?'

'You ask me,' Tulley said. 'we better take it somewhere and burn it. No clues then.'

'Oh sure.' Starke spoke sarcastically. 'A great idea. And then we just walk away. Is that it? Just take a good look at things and tell me we're not in the shit. How much cash did you get?'

'Can't say exactly. A good wad. Got blood on some of it.'

'And you hope people won't notice when you pay for things? Cut my finger. Sorry about that.'

'Well it can't be helped now. We gotta live with it.'

'Except Slim maybe.'

'Ah, leave it out, cancher?' Harker said.

It was obvious that he had no wish to be reminded of his own mortality.

27

Luck

Kimberley had been waiting for them with some trepidation.

She knew for what purpose they had gone out and she knew the risks involved. She had been afraid that something might go wrong, and when she saw Harker being almost carried into the house she knew how right she had been to be nervous. There was so much blood, it scared her sick.

'Oh, my God! What happened?'

Starke told her, making no attempt to disguise the seriousness of the situation.

'It was a balls-up. This bastard here got hisself stabbed with a pair of scissors and shot the old man what done it to him.'

Her eyes widened. 'You mean killed him?'

'Too true, girlie. And now we're all involved. Except you, of course. Though maybe they could even pin something on you too, as an accessory. I don't know.'

She looked even more scared. 'But I wasn't there.'

'No, you wasn't. But they might say you

241

knew all about it and didn't do nothing to prevent it. Like telling the coppers.'

'Oh, for Pete's sake,' Tulley said. 'Stop trying to scare the kid. We gotta decide what to do now. The way I look at it, we better get to hell outa here pretty damn quick. Because as soon as our dear friend DCI Cartwright gets word of what happened at that there shop the coppers are going to be down here in droves.'

'Why should that happen?' Starke said.

'Stands to reason, don't it? The robbery took place on his manor and we're bound to be chief suspects. We might've been anyway, but if things had gone right they wouldn't have had the evidence. Now things are different. A dead man in the shop, blood all over the place — in the shop, in the car, on Slim's clothes. Not to mention a wopping great cut in his side. You don't reckon they'll think all that a mite suspicious?'

This brought their attention back to Harker, who was sitting on a chair and looking a very sick man indeed.

'Better get a dressing on that before he loses more blood.'

Starke's expression seemed to indicate that it would not have bothered him if Harker had bled to death. In Starke's estimation he was entirely to blame for the situation they now found themselves in.

But Tulley and the girl were more sympathetic, and a sheet was torn up and after the victim had been stripped to the skin and the nasty-looking wound had been cleaned up to some extent with water and Dettol, a pad was applied and a few layers of not very clean linen were wrapped round his waist to hold it in position. Blood still seeped through, but in smaller quantities, and the hope was that eventually it would cease to flow.

Harker was not a good patient, and complained all the time he was being attended to.

'By rights I oughter be in hospital.'

'By rights you oughter be in a cell,' Starke said. 'Quit moaning. Else we may leave you here.'

* * *

They were on the move with as little delay as possible, afraid that the upholders of the law might arrive there before they left. They took most of what little gear they had, stowed in the boot of the Renault. They took the banknotes too; those with blood on them as well as those that were relatively clean. The total was just one hundred and sixty-five pounds, with another three pounds and fifty-five pence in small change. Perhaps it had been a poor day's trading for Mr Patel. It had certainly been an unfortunate one for him in other respects.

They decided to head for the country. Their plans were vague. The main object was to get away from the house, where they might find themselves trapped.

'Maybe we can find a hideaway,' Tulley said. 'Sleep in the car.'

'And after that?' Starke said

Tulley had not had any thoughts beyond that point. Whatever plan they might make, Harker was going to be the handicap. Wherever they went he would be conspicuous. Starke was of the opinion that they should just dump him, but he did not say so. Secretly, he hoped the man would die. It would solve one problem. He had also been dubious about taking the girl. He said she would be in the way. But she begged them not to leave her, and Tulley voted in her favour and got his way. Harker was far too concerned with his own troubles to care one way or the other.

So they all set off, Starke driving and Tulley sitting beside him, while Kimberley rode in the back with the injured Harker. The rear seat had been cleaned as much as possible and an old blanket had been spread over it to cover the bloodstains.

As soon as they were clear of outer London they took to the minor roads, heading into the Essex countryside. The time was getting on for eleven o'clock and there had been no sign of any pursuit or of road-blocks being set up. The rain was still falling, but it was no more than a heavy drizzle. The road ahead looked black and shining like molten tar in the light of the headlamps, and there was little traffic. Tulley said: 'Looks like they haven't got on to us yet. So we're in luck so far.'

'We'll need a sight more than luck,' Starke said.

He seemed determined to look on the black side of things; and a little later he remarked sourly: 'We're running out of petrol. Do you know that?'

Tulley had not been watching the fuel gauge. Now he looked at it and saw that Starke was right. It was quite a while since they had had the tank filled, and the journey from London had used up most of what was left.

'We'll have to stop at the next garage and get a fill-up.'

'On this road? What a hope! Most of the villages don't have pumps these days, and everybody's likely to have gone to bed anyway.'

'Better get back to a main road then.'

'If we can. You know the nearest way?'

'Let's have a look at the map.'

Starke brought the car to a halt, and Tulley unfolded the map and studied it with the aid of the interior light. When he had done so he was not hopeful.

'Seems to me if we take the next turn to the left we'll find a B road about twenty miles further on. But then we'd probably have miles more to go before we'd find a garage.'

'So we're buggered,' Starke said. 'We should've got a fill-up before leaving the Smoke.'

'Of course we should. But none of us thought of it, did we? So now we gotta think of something else.'

'Like what?'

'Like maybe getting ourselves another car.'

'Oh, great! And how do we do that?'

Tulley gave him an outline of the plan that had come into his head. It was a fairly simple one, and Starke had to agree that it might work. Harker had taken no part in the discussion. He was completely absorbed by his own personal trouble. He had this terrible pain in his side and he felt sick. He wondered whether he was going to die; and the possibility terrified him.

Starke got the car moving again, driving slowly and keeping an eye on his side of the road while Tulley watched the other. It was Tulley who spotted the gateway and told Starke to stop the car.

'This should do.'

There was a tall thorn hedge which looked as though it had not been trimmed for some years. It had grown to a height of about nine or ten feet and it enclosed a field in which was growing some kind of root crop which could have been sugar beet. There was a gateway with a rickety old five-barred gate which was certainly well past its best days. Tulley and Starke had to lift it to get it open. Then Starke drove the Renault into the field and hid it from sight behind the overgrown hedge.

'The question is,' Starke said, 'will there be another car using this road at this time of night? We haven't seen much traffic.'

'So we'll just have to hope for the best,' Tulley said.

'While fearing the worst.'

'If you want to.'

They were on a fairly straight length of road, and if any vehicle were to come along it would signal its approach fairly early by its headlights. The trouble was that for a time nothing did come. And when eventually something did it turned out to be a lorry, which was not what they were looking for.

It was another half-hour before a car came along. They saw its lights shining through the continuing drizzle of rain, and they could tell by the sound that it was no lorry this time. It could have been a pick-up truck or a light van, but they hoped for the best.

Tulley spoke to the girl. 'You know what to do?'

'Yes.'

She was nervous but ready to play her part in the operation.

'Get going then.'

She stepped out into the road while Tulley and Starke remained hidden behind the hedge. Tulley had the revolver in his hand. Harker had been left in the Renault, since he was out of action.

It had been Tulley's idea that Kim should be used as a decoy. She was to stand in the road and signal to the driver of the approaching car to stop. People were chary of giving lifts to strangers these days, especially at night. So many of them turned out to be villains. But a girl in distress would hardly appear dangerous.

So there she was in the rain waving her arms as the car drew nearer, and for a moment Tulley, peering through the hedge, feared it was going to run her down. But however scared she might have been, she stood her ground and the car came to a halt with a screech of tyres just a few feet away from her.

That was when Tulley and Starke emerged from the field.

They saw then that the car was a fairly new one. It was a Fiat hatchback with plenty of room inside. At the moment it appeared to be pretty crowded with young men and women. Tulley guessed they had been having a night out and were all a little tipsy, including the driver. They must have been surprised to see Tulley and Starke suddenly appear out of the darkness. But it was not worrying them. At first.

Tulley spoke to the driver, who had opened the door on his side and was gaping at him.

'This is where you all get out.'

'Are you crazy?' the man said.

'No. We just need a car, and this one will do nicely.'

The driver turned to the others in the car. 'You hear that? He wants our car.'

They all had a good laugh at that. It seemed to be a great joke.

Tulley showed the revolver to the driver. 'We're not fooling. You better believe it.'

The man, who looked as if he might well have fitted into a rugby scrum, seemed unimpressed. 'What is that? A toy? Go and play your games somewhere else.'

'You think this is a toy?' Tulley said. 'Think again.'

He fired the revolver at a distant part of the road and they could all hear the screech of the ricochet.

It had a miraculous sobering effect on all of them. When he pointed the gun at them and told them to get out of the car they came tumbling out as fast as they could. He herded them into a group at the rear while Starke and the girl fetched their gear from the Renault and transferred it to the Fiat. Last of all they helped the groaning Harker to get himself onto one of the rear seats. The entire operation had taken less than ten minutes. Then they were away with Starke driving.

Tulley looked at the fuel gauge.

'We're in luck. The tank's nearly full.'

'It'll take more than that to get us out of the fix we're in,' Starke said.

He seemed determined to be depressed, come what might.

28

Chase

Detetective Chief Inspector Stephen Cartwright was sleeping peacefully in bed with his
wife when he was unceremoniously snatched
away from any pleasant dreams he might have
been enjoying by the clangour of the
telephone bell. He was still half asleep when
he picked up the instrument.

'Cartwright here.'

The information that came through to him
brought him fully awake in an instant. It
concerned a raid on a shop owned by a Mr
Patel. It had been a bungled affair, during
which the shop-keeper himself had been shot
dead and his wife assaulted.

'I'll be right there,' Cartwright said.

He glanced at the bedside clock and saw
that the time was coming up to midnight. He
wondered at what time the raid had taken
place. It must surely have been much earlier
than that. And if so, why had the information
taken so long to reach him?

The fact of the matter was that the crime
could have been reported much earlier if the

man with the umbrella at whom Tulley had pointed his gun had not been so determined not to become involved. He had thought about calling the police, since it was evident that a crime had been committed. But then he had thought again and had decided that it was none of his business. So he just went home and said nothing.

As a result of this lack of public spirit in a member of the community, the crime was destined to go unreported until the unfortunate Mrs Patel regained consciousness and managed to give a somewhat incoherent report of what had happened after dialling 999.

Cartwright lost no time in getting to the scene of the incident, and to him it looked very much like a botched job. And from there he had no hesitation in turning his thoughts to the gang of three villains whose actions had been much on his mind for some time past. As a consequence of this, a strong body of police, some armed, descended on the house in which the three had been living for some time, in company latterly with a young prostitute.

They arrived too late. The birds had flown.

But Cartwright knew the old Renault they were using for transport these days and the registration number was on record. This was immediately circulated, together with a warning that the occupants of the car might be armed and dangerous.

By this time, however, unknown to Cartwright, the Renault had been dumped and the fugitives had transferred themselves to a Fiat. It was quite a while before this information filtered through, along with the number of the new getaway vehicle; and by then the car was hidden in a wood with the girl and two of the men sleeping inside it. The third man, Harker, was finding sleep hard to come by. He was sick and in pain and feeling very sorry for himself.

★   ★   ★

It was getting on for nine o'clock in the morning by the time they were all awake. The rain had moved away during the night, and it was a fine, bright day with the sun shining. It was the kind of day that might have been calculated to raise the spirits, but it would have taken more than a change in the weather to produce such a transformation in any member of the little party in the Fiat. They were in trouble and they knew it.

They were also hungry and thirsty.

'We'll have to get some grub somewhere,' Tulley said. 'We can't just live on fresh air.'

Which was stating the obvious.

'So what do we do?' Starke said. 'It's likely the fuzz have got the number of this car by now. So wherever we go in it will be taking a risk.'

'We could leave it here and walk to the nearest village. Find a pub or something.'

'We'd attract attention.'

'Not as much as a car with a sick man inside and a girl with a scarred face.'

'We oughter dumped that bastard Slim ages ago,' Starke said. 'It's him what's got us into this mess. First he puts a slug into Chuck Brogan's noggin when he's our best lead to the gold. Then he knocks off the old Paki in his shop and gets hisself stabbed with a pair of scissors. Now we're stuck with him. Can't even leave him outside a hospital because it might put the coppers onto us.'

'They're onto us anyway,' Tulley said. 'You can be sure of that.'

★ ★ ★

In the end they decided that he and Starke should take a walk to see if they could find a village or a public house, leaving the girl with Harker. Neither she nor he were very happy with this arrangement, but the other two were not happy either; so it added up to

254

four unhappy people.

In one way Tulley and Starke were lucky. They had not walked more than half a mile when they came to a crossroads with a signpost. The nearest place marked on it was one and a half miles away and went by the name of Sutton-cum-Crawley. There was of course no indication of how large it was, but they decided to try it. Neither of them did much walking as a rule and they were not enjoying the exercise. There was quite a bit of traffic on the road now, but no one stopped to offer them a lift, and they made no attempt to thumb one.

At Sutton-cum-Crawley they were again in luck. Unlike so many villages nowadays, it still boasted a post office and general store. There they bought some cheese and biscuits, four packets of crisps and a few cans of Pepsi-Cola. The elderly woman who served them asked no questions, though she looked as if she might have liked to. She gave them a couple of used polythene bags to carry their purchases in and told them to have a nice day.

Tulley could think of nothing about it that was likely to be nice except maybe the weather, but he did not say so.

* * *

The girl was relieved to see them back at the place where they had left the car. She said nobody had been in the wood, but she believed Harker was getting worse.

'He's been singing.'

Tulley stared at her. 'Singing?'

'Yes. All nonsense and not much tune. I think he's delirious at times. He's beginning to stink too.'

'That's nothing,' Starke said. 'He always did stink.'

★   ★   ★

They made a meal with the stuff they had brought from the shop, though Harker ate nothing. He seemed to have a great thirst though, and would have drunk far more than his share of the cans of Pepsi if he had been allowed to do so. He did some more of the singing that the girl had described, and Starke threatened to strangle him if he didn't put a sock in it.

Soon after that he either went to sleep or sank into a coma. They were not sure which.

'You ask me,' Starke said, 'we're going to have a dead man on our hands before we're finished. What we do then?'

Nobody answered that one. The bandage covering Harker's injury was stiff with dried blood. None of them knew what was going on under the dressing, and they were not feeling inclined to take a look.

They discussed what their next move should be. Tulley suggested they should stay where they were until after dark.

'Nobody's been here so far, and with luck nobody will find us. They won't be looking in a place like this.'

He was probably right about that. They had driven into the wood along an old track that looked as though it had not been used for quite a while, and they were completely hidden from the road. The car had left wheel-marks, but these were not conspicuous and nobody was likely to notice them from a passing vehicle; and why would they bother to investigate anyway? The car was nowhere near the place where it had been stolen.

'And then?' Starke said.

'Then I suggest we head north,' Tulley said.

He really had no reason for the suggestion, but he could think of nothing better. Obviously they could not stay where they were indefinitely, and going north was as good as anything else.

★   ★   ★

It was getting on for midnight when they set out. And it was just twenty minutes later when the police car got on their tail and signalled to them to stop.

'No way,' Starke said.

He put his foot down on the accelerator and the Fiat responded with a nice turn of speed. The police car was fast too, and it hung on, siren blaring. They sped through one village where no one appeared to be stirring and came out onto a narrow and winding country road with no other traffic on it.

The girl was scared. She had never been in a car chase before and she was not enjoying the experience. She had fastened her seat belt, but Tulley and Starke had not bothered with theirs. It was just one more regulation to ignore, and there would be far more serious offences to take into account if they were caught.

'The bastard's still on our tail,' Tulley said. 'He's hanging on.'

Starke snarled back at him: 'Now tell me something I don't know.'

He forced a little more speed out of the Fiat, came to another bend in the road and took it with a screech of tyres.

The roadblock was dead ahead. It had been set up in a strategic position: on one side of the parked police cars was a steep bank with a hedge on top, while on the other side was an oak tree that had probably been there for centuries.

Starke kept his foot on the accelerator, not reducing speed at all. He must have decided that he could batter one of the police cars aside and force a way between it and the oak. He was wrong. The Fiat bounced off the stationary car and hit the tree head-on. Tulley and Starke were flung out of their seats and their skulls were crushed against the windscreen. They died instantly.

The car was so wrecked that it had to be cut open to get at the people inside. It was discovered then that there was a third dead man on the rear seat, but they could not be certain that he had died in the crash or whether he had already been dead as the result of a considerable loss of blood from a gash in his side.

There was a girl too. She was alive but unconscious. When they lifted her out a young constable remarked that she might have been quite an attractive kid if it had not been for the disfiguring scars on her cheeks.

When she came to and they told her how lucky she had been to have survived the smash, all she said was:

'I wish I was dead.'

And she sounded as though she really meant it.

29

Bingo Again

Alan Caley's financial situation was going from bad to worse. He had been seduced by one of the offers that kept coming through his letter box to take out a loan for five thousand pounds, the property being security for this amount.

But already the money was nearly all gone. For a start, Martine had come again with her begging-bowl, and she had taken a thousand off him straightaway. How she had managed it he still could not quite understand. He should never have told her about the loan; he could see that now. But he had, and she had latched onto it at once, saying that he really owed her more than that, because, after all, she was still his wife and he was responsible for providing her with a decent allowance.

He might have argued that, since she had walked out on him of her own accord, she was entitled to nothing, because she was performing no wifely duties. But he was reluctant to say anything that might encourage her to come back. He doubted whether she would, but he was afraid to take the risk, since she just might do it if she was having trouble with her parents. So the thousand pounds had really been a kind of danegeld; a bribe to keep her away from him.

Things were made worse by the fact that some demands had come in for bills that had been overlooked; so that now there was very little of the five thousand pounds left.

The only bright spot on his present horizon was the news that the three criminals, Tulley, Harker and Starke, were dead. It was a great relief to know that they would never again come to plague him with their demands to be told where Brogan had stashed the gold. Now, if only he could find it, all would be fine. Unfortunately, he had failed in that quest and all was very far from fine.

And yet it had to be lying around somewhere, and it was hard to believe that Brogan's cryptic map did not provide the clue to where the hiding-place was. He must surely have missed something. For the map had to hold the secret if only he could work it out. What other possible reason could there have been for the man to draw it and confide it with so much care to him — Alan Caley?

He took it out and examined it again. And yet again he felt convinced that he had worked out the puzzle correctly. The triangle of country roads, the names of the villages, the trees marking the spot — he had surely identified all these correctly.

'I can't have got it wrong,' he muttered. 'I can't.'

So what had happened to the trees?

Suppose they had been cut down.

Oddly enough, this possibility had simply never occurred to him until that moment. And of course it put a completely new complexion on the whole affair. Suddenly hope came to life again. The business was not finished yet; not by a long chalk.

But then he reflected that if they had been cut down the stumps would have been rooted out and the gold would have been discovered. And this had certainly not happened. So perhaps the stumps had been left. He had seen none, but he had not been looking for any, and they might have been hidden by tall grass.

The more he thought about it, the more he was taken by the idea. Now he would certainly go down there again and take another look. He lit a cigarette and drew smoke into his lungs and felt quite elated. It was almost as if his troubles had been put to flight and the gold was in his hands.

Then another idea came to him. Why not buy a metal detector and use it to locate the gold? He thought about this for some time, but finally rejected it. He had never used one of those things, and he did not think it would be necessary anyway. He would find the stuff now. He was sure of it.

'I'm going to be rich. I'm going to be rich.'

Reaction set in later, and the euphoria faded. Was he building too much on this new possibility? It was, after all, only a theory. But still he felt that it must be right, for what other explanation could there be for the vanishing trees? They had been there when Brogan had buried the gold, but then he had spent all those years forcibly restrained from going to claim his prize. Much could have happened in the interim, and then at the last he had been robbed of his reward by one small piece of baser metal from Harker's gun.

It had been an injustice of course; but the world was full of injustices, and at least Harker and his henchmen had not lived to profit by this crime. And now they could not even threaten him. Indeed, it was all working out to his advantage. At last the great wheel of fortune was turning in his favour.

★ ★ ★

He set out early next morning, and it looked like being a fine, bright day; which he took to be a good omen. He had the spade which had so interested Detective Sergeant Brown in the back of the pick-up truck with the tilt covering it; and he made the journey down into Norfolk in better time than he had on the previous occasion. He knew the way now, and by midday he had reached what in his mind he felt he might call the golden triangle.

He went immediately to the village named Kenthorpe, approaching it from the South Wootton side, and then drove slowly along the road leading out of it in the direction of Inglewood. As he did so he made an examination of the fields on his left, for somewhere in one of those fields there should have been three silver birches, maybe some fifty yards or so in from the road. There were none now of course, and he could see no tree stumps either. Moreover, there was no long grass to hide their presence for quite a distance because there was one big meadow. There were horses grazing on it and it was enclosed by a post and rail fence, as he should have remembered from his first visit, but had not.

It was a bitter disappointment for Caley. He had been so confident of finding tree stumps that he had even pictured them in his mind. And now he realised that he had been deceiving himself, that this new hope had been nothing but an illusion, a chimera, conjured up to fool him. How could he have been such a fool?

He turned the truck and drove slowly back towards the village. He noticed that there were three large houses some hundred yards or so from where the main village street began. These three appeared to be of fairly recent construction, and each was well separated from the other two. They were the kind that might at today's inflated prices have sold for some four or five hundred thousand pounds each. There were fairly large gardens at the back enclosed by larch wood fencing.

Caley had taken very little notice of them when he had passed them before, but now something caught his eye in the gap between the middle house and the one furthest from the village. It looked like the branch of a tree.

Something seemed to bubble up inside him. Could it be that he had found what he had been seeking? Could it possibly be that?

He stopped the truck and backed it until it was level with the gap between the two houses; and when he had reached a certain point he could see, not just one branch but an entire tree.

And the tree was a silver birch.

Bingo again!

He had little doubt that, were he to go to

the rear of the middle house, he would discover that at the far end of the garden were three silver birches that had been left standing when the house was built. And he had no doubt either that close to the roots of those birches was the cache of gold that Chuck Brogan had buried there.

So Bingo yet again!

An elderly man on an elderly bicycle was trundling down the road. Caley got out of the pick-up truck and hailed him. The elderly man came to a halt and descended from his machine with care.

'Excuse me,' Caley said. 'I wonder whether you could tell me how long it is since these houses were built?'

The cyclist stared at Caley with a calculating but somewhat rheumy eye.

'Ain't for sale, you know.'

'Oh,' Caley said, 'I wasn't thinking of buying one. I just wondered how old they were. They look fairly new.'

'All built about the same time as I recall. Reckon as how that'd be gettin' on for four year ago. No more.'

Caley's heart leaped again. Brogan had been safely stowed away behind locked doors well before any start had been made on the houses. The land on which they were built could still have been part of the field at the back, waiting to be developed.

'Do you know who's living in that middle one?'

The elderly man scratched his head, lifting a somewhat threadbare cloth cap in order to do so.

'Can't rightly say. Ain't bin there long. Tother one went away. They do say as how his wife up and left him; but that may be just gossip. Folks will talk.'

Caley thanked him for his information and the man mounted his bicycle and pedalled away, long legs moving like pistons.

When he had gone Caley turned the truck again and drove until he was out of sight of the houses before parking on the grass verge, lighting a cigarette and giving some thought to the situation. One thing was certain: he could not walk into a man's garden and start digging a hole in broad daylight. The operation would have to wait until he felt sure that everyone in the house had gone to bed. And that would certainly not be before midnight.

It would, he thought, be best to launch his attack from the rear. He could leave the truck not too far up the road, since he would have a number of bars of gold to carry to it, and these were likely to be heavy. However, he would have several hours in which to do the job; and did it matter if it made him sweat? It would be well worth the labour.

He had no doubt that he could get into the garden without much difficulty. He would go round to the back of the house by way of the meadow. There would be two fences to climb over — the post and rail one that enclosed the pasture and the four-foot panel one that belonged to the owner of the house. If the two were close enough together he might use the one to help him climb over the other.

He had had the foresight to bring some provisions with him, since he did not wish to show himself in a public house. He would take the truck a good distance away from the village and maybe get some sleep in the cab; though this might not prove easy to come by in his present excited state.

Nevertheless, in the event he did doze off for an hour or two after it grew dark, and he awoke with the fear that he might have slept too long and lost the chance of carrying out the operation that night. However, a glance at his wristwatch with the aid of the interior light reassured him. It was still only ten o'clock.

He had found a driftway leading to a disused gravel pit, and this had served splendidly to conceal the truck while he waited. Now he took some refreshment, smoked a number of cigarettes, and at a little after midnight was on his way.

30

No Justice

There were no lights showing in any of the three houses when he took the truck onto the grass verge beside the post-and-rail fence and switched off the lights of the vehicle also.

It was a night well suited to the operation he was about to carry out. There was a sliver of moon in a thinly clouded sky, giving enough light for him to find his way as soon as his eyes had become accustomed to it.

He took the spade from the back of the truck and climbed over the fence into the meadow. He was startled by an indistinct shape coming up and snorting at him. But then he realised it was one of the horses, and a moment later it had galloped away with a thudding of hooves.

A little later he had reached the place where he could make out the shadowy form of the three silver birches. He moved closer to them and climbed to the top rail of the meadow fence. From there it was quite easy to step across to the top of the other one, which was only four feet high, and then jump down into the garden. Unfortunately, the posts supporting this second fence had rotted at ground level, and as he was about to jump the section on which he was standing gave way with a loud cracking noise which sounded to the startled intruder like a clap of thunder. He himself, spade in hand, was thrown to the ground.

It was a fall softened by the closely mown turf on which he landed, but he was fearful that the noise he had made would rouse whoever was asleep in the house, or even in the adjacent houses. So for a while he stayed where he was, listening for the sound of any alarm. But nothing came, and the breaking of the fence seemed only to have aroused a dog which was barking some distance away.

After a while Caley stood up, grasped the spade and set to work on the task of digging up the garden of a perfect stranger. He decided that it would be of no use digging close to the trees, since the roots would have prevented Brogan from burying his horde there. All that part of the garden appeared to have been laid down as a lawn, so he imagined that no one would have done any deep digging there to plant shrubs or bushes. It had probably been left undisturbed since it had been turfed or sown with grass seed after the house was built. Brogan would surely have dug pretty deeply to ensure that the gold was not discovered. And he had been successful in that respect, for if it had been found Cartwright would have got to know about it and would not still be searching.

Caley had not done much digging in his life, but he set about his task with a will. He dug for two hours, maybe getting on for three. He was sweating heavily and his hands were blistered. He must have covered half the lawn according to his calculation. He was now at least twenty yards from the trees. And he had found nothing.

It occurred to him that perhaps after all he ought to have bought a metal detector. But he did not believe even that would have been of any use. He had reluctantly come to the conclusion that no gold had ever been there. He had been misled by Brogan's sketch map, either because he had deciphered it incorrectly or because it had all along been nothing more than a hoax. The fact might have been that those years spent in prison had warped Chuck's brain. Perhaps in fact he had himself forgotten where he had hidden the gold. Whatever the truth of the matter was, one thing now appeared certain: it was not in this garden.

Reluctantly Caley decided that he had to accept this unpalatable fact. It was a bitter end to all his fond hopes, but there was no escaping the truth that ever since the death of Chuck Brogan he had been living with a grand illusion — the belief that he would eventually be led to a fortune by a scrap of paper. Now he knew that he was just the owner of some crumbling property, living on borrowed money and harassed by an estranged and demanding wife.

He could not yet see any sign that dawn was breaking, but he had had enough. He picked up the spade, stepped over the wreckage of the garden fence, got himself over the one enclosing the meadow and made his weary way back to the pick-up truck.

He thought of going straight back to London; but he was just too worn out by his nocturnal labours to face the journey without first having some rest. So he drove the truck away from the vicinity of the houses, parked it again by an overgrown hedge and went to sleep.

★ ★ ★

The sun was shining when he awoke, and a glance at his watch revealed the fact that it was getting on for half-past nine. His hands were sore, his whole body ached and he felt horribly dirty. Recollection of his unsuccessful late night activities added to a feeling of deep depression.

He was hungry, and he made a makeshift breakfast of what was left of his provisions. He decided then that before returning to London he would take one last look at the place where his rural expedition had come to its dismal conclusion. So he started the engine, turned the truck and drove back to the three houses.

★ ★ ★

He could see at once that there was a little group of three men in front of the middle house. They appeared to be in conference, and he felt that he could guess what they were talking about. He felt an urge to hear what they were saying; so he brought the truck to a halt and got out.

The men fell silent as he walked towards them and stared at him with curiosity. He saw that two of them were middle-aged and the third much younger.

'I wonder,' he said, 'whether you could tell me if I'm on the right road to a place called South Wootton?'

One of the older men answered: 'You are. It's not far. Couple of miles or so.'

'Thank you,' Caley said. Then added:

'Early morning conference?'

The question seemed to act like a spur to the younger man; and it was immediately apparent that he was the owner of the middle house. The other two were probably his neighbours.

'I've been telling these gentlemen about something that happened in the night. Unbelievable, quite unbelievable.'

'Oh? What was that?'

'Some lunatic or criminal broke my garden fence down and dug up most of my lawn. Must have been at it for hours. And why? For what purpose? That's what I'd like to know.'

'Devilment,' one of the other men suggested. 'May have been more than one, of course. Vandals.'

'I've only had the property for a couple of weeks or so,' the younger man said. 'And the odd thing is that it was rather like that when I moved in. There was this big hole in the middle of the lawn, like it might have been dug for a cesspit or something. The rest of it was just neglected — rough grass and weeds. I had the whole lot returfed. Cost the devil of a lot, I can tell you. Now I'll need to have it all done again.'

Caley was feeling sick. He was beginning to see why his labour of the night had been in vain; why there had been nothing to dig up.

Someone had been there before him. Someone had taken his gold, almost from under his nose. It was enough to make anyone sick.

'This man you bought the place from. What was he like?'

'No idea. Never met him. Sale was all arranged by agents and solicitors. Why do you ask?'

He was looking at Caley with a certain interest, and Caley had an uneasy feeling that there was too much evidence of his nocturnal labours on his shoes and on his hands.

'No reason,' he said hurriedly. 'Just thought he might have told you how it came to be dug up the first time.'

One of the other men, who was wearing a green cardigan, put a word in then. 'Name of Danby. Good-looking young chap. Well off, I'd say. Had some kind of business in Norwich; never heard exactly what it was. Kept a yacht somewhere on the coast and did a lot of sailing. Long distance stuff. Sometimes away for months on end. Wife never went with him. Left to her own devices. Then just before he sold the place she walked out on him. Leastways, that's the story going around.'

'That would be why he sold the property, would it?'

'Could've been, I suppose.'

The other older man chipped in then: 'Ah, but there was more to it than that. There was this dolly girl, wasn't there?'

'Dolly girl?' Caley said.

'Yes. One day he turns up with her. She'd be a lot younger than him, and a real eye-catcher. She stayed the night, but next morning they went away and never came back. Some men turned up later with a furniture van and cleared the things out of the house.'

'You don't know where the man and the girl went?'

'No idea.'

The one who had spoken before now volunteered some more information. 'I had a chat with him a day or two earlier. He didn't usually do much in that line, but this time he just seemed inclined to talk. I don't know why. In the mood, I reckon. He was in high spirits too; I could see that. Anyway, he told me a bit about himself and what he was planning.'

'And what was that?'

'A trip to Brazil.'

'Ah!'

'And then this girl appears and the next day they're gone. So what do you make of that?'

Caley was making quite a lot of it, and not liking the result one little bit.

'How long before this was it when his garden was dug up? Do you know?'

'Just a few days, I'd say. I happened to be on a ladder clearing some rubbish out of the gutter, and I could see into his garden. I thought then it seemed to be in a mess.'

'Not as bad as this time though,' the younger man said. 'There was just the one big hole; it wasn't dug up all over. And the fence wasn't broken down.'

Which confirmed Caley's worst fears.

The man in the green cardigan said: 'I don't think they'll be coming back.'

'Did he tell you that?' Caley asked.

'Not in so many words. It's just an impression I got. Could be wrong, of course.'

But Caley did not think he was wrong. For why would a man with a fortune in gold bullion and a dolly girl half his age for a companion ever want to come back?

And it was all so unfair. For what had this fellow Danby ever done to earn his windfall? Nothing. While he, Alan Caley, had worked out the meaning of the cryptic sketch map given him by Chuck Brogan, had risked the enmity of a gang of violent criminals, had withstood interrogation from a pair of disbelieving police officers, and in the end had got nothing at all for his pains.

He felt like crying out in agony, as if from some terrible physical wound.

Really, there was no justice in the world. No justice at all.

31

Loser

Detective Chief Inspector Cartwright was on the telephone in his office when Detective Sergeant Brown gave a knock on the door and walked in.

Cartwright put the phone down, and Brown could tell merely by looking at him that he was bursting with some information to impart. And it came without delay.

'Bill, my son. I have great news for you. The gold has been found.'

Brown had no need to ask what gold. There was only one lot of the precious yellow metal that was of interest to the pair of them.

So he just said: 'Where?'

Cartwright grinned at him; positively grinned. Which was so unusual as to be almost unprecedented.

'You won't believe this.'

'Try me,' Brown said.

The grin became a positive smirk. 'Two thousand miles out in the Atlantic Ocean.'

'I don't believe it,' Brown said.

'I told you so.'

'But how — ?'

'There was this little sailing boat, see. Apparently it had been drifting for quite a time after being dismasted in a freak storm. There was an auxiliary engine, but the fuel soon ran out, so that was no help. As luck would have it, there was this frigate of the Royal Navy returning from some kind of duty in the Caribbean. The yacht was picked up on the radar screen and they went to its aid. Party went on board and found a man named Oliver Danby and a girl named Angela Crowe.'

'Aha!'

'Odd thing was they hadn't sent out a mayday call. He was trying to rig a jurymast, whatever that may be, and wasn't terribly grateful for the assistance.'

'No?'

'No. Especially when an officer came on board and discovered a lot of gold ingots hidden away,'

'Our gold?'

'I think we may bet on that.'

'So what's this Oliver Danby's story?'

'Now here's something else that may take some believing. He says there was this mongrel dog used to come into his garden and do a lot of digging; the way dogs do. Then one day it dug a lot deeper than usual and uncovered you know what.'

'Smart dog. We should all have one. So then I suppose our man got to work and dug up the rest of the hoard. Which of course he regarded as his because it was found on his property.'

'Something like that.'

'Do you think the law boys will take the same view?'

'I doubt it,' Cartwright said. 'I very much doubt it.'

And then Brown said: 'I wonder whether our Mr Alan Caley knows about this.'

'If he doesn't already, he soon will,' Cartwright said. 'He'll be sick. He'll be as sick as a toad.'

'And in his shoes, wouldn't you?'

'I wonder just what it was Brogan told him.'

'Now that's the question, isn't it?'

'Whatever it was, it did him no good.'

'In a way, you know, I feel sorry for the poor bastard. He's been a loser all along the line.'

'Somebody has to be,' Brown said. 'We can't all be winners.'

Which perhaps was no more than a statement of the obvious. And would have been no consolation to the loser himself — no consolation at all.

We do hope that you have enjoyed reading this large print book.

Did you know that all of our titles are available for purchase?

We publish a wide range of high quality large print books including:
Romances, Mysteries, Classics
General Fiction
Non Fiction and Westerns

Special interest titles available in large print are:
The Little Oxford Dictionary
Music Book
Song Book
Hymn Book
Service Book

Also available from us courtesy of Oxford University Press:
Young Readers' Dictionary
(large print edition)
Young Readers' Thesaurus
(large print edition)

For further information or a free brochure, please contact us at:
Ulverscroft Large Print Books Ltd.,
The Green, Bradgate Road, Anstey,
Leicester, LE7 7FU, England.
Tel: (00 44) **0116 236 4325**
Fax: (00 44) **0116 234 0205**

Other titles published by
The House of Ulverscroft:

THE GOLDEN REEF

James Pattinson

When the S.S. *Southern Queen* encountered a lifeboat in the Pacific Ocean, a strange mystery was uncovered. For the lifeboat was marked *Valparaiso I* and the *Valparaiso* had been sunk by a Japanese submarine in January 1945, nearly a year earlier. Moreover, the *Valparaiso* had been carrying a million pounds' worth of gold bullion. There was a man in the lifeboat, but his memory had gone — or so he claimed. When he showed an unaccountable desire some years later to return to the Pacific, two other survivors from the *Valparaiso* decided to keep on eye on him, because a million pounds in gold bullion is worth anybody's time and, if necessary, more than a little violence.

THE ANGRY ISLAND

James Pattinson

When Guy Radford goes to visit an old college friend on the West Indian island of St Marien, he is blissfully unaware of the trouble he is flying into. Divisions of race and wealth have created such tensions between desperate workers and powerful plantation owners that a violent showdown is inevitable. When Radford unwittingly becomes caught in the crossfire, he finds his own life in danger. And, as the conflict intensifies, the fact that he has fallen in love adds merely one more complication to an already tricky situation . . .

THE SILENT VOYAGE

James Pattinson

World War Two has ended a few years earlier and the Cold War is starting when Brett Manning is sent to do some business in Archangel. But on his way, in the thick fog and darkness of the Barents Sea, his ship is run down by a much larger vessel. Only Brett and one other man are picked up, and they now find themselves on board a Russian freighter bound for a secret destination. Slowly it dawns on Brett and his companion that they now know too much for their own good and that their very lives are in danger. But how does one escape from a ship at sea?

CRANE

James Pattinson

Paul Crane had not altogether liked the look of Skene and West when they turned up at his north Norfolk cottage and made him an offer he could not refuse, but his chequered past had taught him not to be particular. Down on his luck since eighteen, when he was picked up on Liverpool Street Station by the decidedly odd Heathcliff, Crane promptly teamed up with a young thief named Charlie Green. Only when he fell in love with Penelope was there any hope of going straight. And perhaps he would have stuck to his promise if the chance of making a million had not dropped into his lap.